D1095168

The Sailor

"Do you ever dream of the sea, Martin?"

"Sometimes." Martin looked perplexed at the sudden change of subject. "Doesn't everyone who's been a sailor?"

"Not like mine." Silas stared down into his coffee. "I have nightmares, Martin. They were just a few at first, and I thought it was guilt for my parents, but now they come every time I sleep. They're so vivid… I dream of the sea, but not like I did when I was a kid, not with the feeling like I wanted to be a sailor."

"How then?" All humor had fled Martin's voice, and his lips were set in a hard line.

"I dream *under* the sea, and I see faces, bloated faces with bulging eyes. They remind me of people I knew as a boy, half-drowned, but not dead." Silas shivered, but not from the chill gusts blowing through the open door. Pointed teeth grinned, webbed hands reaching for him, glowing eyes in the darkness… He couldn't tell Martin those details, of course. Some things you couldn't say aloud if you wanted to stay out of the madhouse. "I wanted to know whether you ever had dreams like that. Dreams of people you knew turned into…something horrible. Voices calling you to join them. We both know the Marsh family's an odd lot. I need to know if this is some family affliction, if I'm going crazy, or if you've ever had any—"

"No." Martin downed his coffee and stood so abruptly his leg jostled the table. "Nope, I never dreamed any such thing, Silas, and you best forget you ever did, too!"

This story represents two of my greatest loves: the sea, and fantastical stories. For the former, I thank my father, who taught me that you could love something that occasionally tried to kill you, and the latter, my mother, who taught me that books are better than television.

Cover illustration by Shane Pierce.

Color insert artwork by Mariusz Gandzel, Stephen Somers, and Jokubas Uogintas.

ISBN: 978-1-63344-322-8
Printed in China.

Fantasy Flight Games
1995 West County Road B2
Roseville, MN 55113
USA

Find out more about Fantasy Flight Games
and our many exciting worlds at

www.FantasyFlightGames.com

An

Novella

The Deep Gate

by Chris A. Jackson

Fantasy Flight Games

Welcome to Arkham

IT IS THE HEIGHT OF THE ROARING TWENTIES. Flappers and young fellas dance the Charleston at raucous jazz clubs gleaming bright with electric lights. Beneath this gilded glamour, bloody turf wars rage, funded by gangsters and crooked cops who frequent rival speakeasies and gambling dens.

Amid these changing times, old New England towns hold their secrets close. Off the Aylesbury pike, in reclusive Dunwich, rolling hills hide decrepit farms and witch-haunted hollows. Past Cape Ann, the remote fishing village of Innsmouth rots from within. At the mouth of the Miskatonic River, mist-shrouded Kingsport lies dreaming. All the while, historic Arkham broods on the upper banks of the Miskatonic, its famed university delving into the world's darkest, most ancient mysteries.

Arkham's citizens insist everything is normal in their sleepy town, but horrific and bizarre events occur with increasing frequency. Strange lights flicker and people disappear in the forest beyond Hangman's Brook. Misshapen silhouettes prowl graveyards and shorelines, leaving savaged corpses in their wake. Nightmarish artifacts and disturbing tomes have surfaced, chronicling gods and incantations the world has tried to forget. Cavalier scientists have glimpsed far-flung worlds beyond our own that shatter the known laws of reality. Are these events somehow connected? If so, what calamity do they portend?

Those who dare investigate these incidents witness the inexplicable. Having seen such phenomena, they can never regain their old view of the world. Now that they know the hideous truth, they cannot run or hide from it. Just beneath the reassuring veneer of reality—a veneer that was never meant to be worn away—are forces that can drive the average person to despair. Yet, a rare few try to avert the end of the world, knowing it may well cost them their lives or sanity.

These investigators must rely on their wits and skills to learn as much as they can before it's too late. Some may find courage in the grace of a rosary, while others may burn away their fears with a swig of bootleg whiskey. They must try their hand at unpredictable spells that could doom them, or take up rifles and revolvers to combat foul creatures plaguing the night. Will it be enough?

Chapter One

Arkham River Docks

Silas squinted through the rain-slashed pilothouse windows as he maneuvered *Sea Change* gingerly toward the Arkham quay wall. The rain-gorged Miskatonic River ran like a millrace, eddies and whirlpools wrenching the small boat about and making an otherwise simple operation tricky. With one hand on the wheel and the other on the throttle, he gunned the engine against a surge of current and eased closer to the tall pilings.

"Come on, dearie, don't fail me now…"

The slogging run up from Kingsport against the flow had taxed the small boat's engine and her captain's nerves to the limit, but the trial wasn't over yet. He had to get a bow line secured without allowing the current to push the boat downriver. A glance over his shoulder at the looming river barge docked just behind verified his worry. One mistake and the current would drag *Sea Change* right under the barge's sloped bow.

"Come on, Silas, you've done this a hundred times…" *Of course, it'd be easier if I could see a damned thing!* He leaned out the pilothouse door, squinted his one good eye against the rain, and ducked back to adjust his speed and course. Bow into the current, running just hard enough to keep from drifting backward, he steered her closer. Finally, he felt the gentle nudge of the rub rail meeting a piling. He tied off the wheel and stepped out onto the foredeck.

Rain plastered his hair flat and ran in rivulets down his bare chest, but Silas barely noticed. Born and raised on the New England shore, he'd swam in the Atlantic in late fall and early spring as a boy. This September nor'easter was certainly blowing like a banshee, but it wasn't promising snow. Besides, people weren't far off when they said he had enough hair on his chest to make a wool sweater blush in shame. He looped a dock line twice around the piling, secured it to the bow cleat, and stepped back into the pilothouse. Wiping the water from his face, Silas pulled the throttle lever all the way back and jerked the gear shift into neutral. The engine all but sighed in relief as it settled to a slow, soothing idle.

"Good girl." He patted the wheel, stepped aft down into the boat's main cabin, and bent to open a hatch in the deck.

Silas blinked through the wave of heat rising up from the thrumming engine. A veteran of both sail and steam, he considered internal combustion engines to be cantankerous beasts prone to unpredictable failure. He'd come to rely on *Sea Change*'s sturdy Knox Model-G with few reservations, but if an engine died at sea or in the turbulent flow of the Miskatonic, he couldn't simply walk to the nearest service station. Consequently, every mariner worth his salt was also a mechanic.

"Hot as a two-dollar pistol," Silas muttered. He left the hatch open to let it cool off before shutting down, happy with the boat's performance if little else. He hadn't wanted to make the trip up to Arkham, but the opportunity to get some answers dragged at him like a sea anchor. He'd returned to New England to find someone who could tell him if his recurrent nightmares were some kind of family malady—like dropsy or ulcers often were—but there seemed to be a pall of silence hanging over everyone he talked to. Every cousin or childhood friend he asked told him they didn't know what he was talking about, or warned him not to let on that he was plagued by nightmares lest he risk getting locked up in the loony bin. A few days ago, however, he'd contacted another relative by telephone and had been encouraged.

Maybe this time I'll finally understand...

Silas strode through the small cabin and out to the aft deck, and then finished securing *Sea Change* to the quay. After decades at sea, serving aboard every manner of vessel from coal-fired steamers to Singapore junks, he knew ships like he knew the scars on his hands. In the few months he'd owned *Sea Change*, he'd come to love the little boat. She was sturdy, comfortable enough to live aboard, and equipped to serve his many needs. The familiar tasks of tending her lines and tidying up the deck settled his nerves, but as he turned back to the cabin to shut down the engine, a booming voice from the pier drew his attention from his chores.

"Silas Marsh, you old sea dog, don't you *ever* wear a shirt?"

Shielding his eye from the rain, Silas squinted up at the figure there. Swathed in slicker and sou'wester, the man's face was cast in shadow, but he recognized the voice easily enough. "Why wear somethin' that's just gonna get soaked through anyway?" He smiled up at his cousin, although the expression felt forced. *Too many sleepless nights, and too many nightmares.* "Come aboard, Martin! I've got a pot of java on the stove."

"Best offer I've had all day!" Martin stepped down onto the deck with practiced ease. The man had been a stevedore, a deck hand, and a longshoreman all over New England, and had only recently settled down in Arkham. "Wicked nor'easter brewin'!"

"They come earlier every year." Silas shook his cousin's hand firmly and waved him into the cabin. "Watch your step. Engine room's open."

Martin and Silas had grown up together in Innsmouth, but that seemed a lifetime ago. Silas left that dismal place for a life at sea when he was but a boy, so Martin undoubtedly knew the oddities of the Marsh family better than he. News of Silas's parents passing two years ago, and now these recurring dreams, had called him inexorably back here. Martin would surely know if Silas's incessant nightmares and the constant yearning he felt to be at sea were some kind of family madness or just guilt for abandoning his parents.

Martin stepped inside, shook out his slicker, and doffed his hat, which he hung on a peg in the wet locker. "Ah, the warm's a welcome, ain't it?"

"If you say so." Silas preferred a cool breeze on the open sea. He waved a hand to the tiny chart table and two bench seats. Atop the adjacent potbelly Franklin stove, a coffee pot secured by fiddles bubbled merrily. "Pour yourself a cup and have a seat while I shut this noisy beast down."

"Thanks!"

Martin pulled two tin cups down from their hooks and filled them while Silas stepped past him, knelt to shut down the engine, and closed the hatch. The rain drumming on the cabin top seemed to amplify in the sudden quiet.

"Can't say I wasn't surprised to get your call, Silas. Haven't seen you since you were barely old enough to shave!" Martin raised his cup and sipped. "Heard you finally gave up the high-seas trade and came home."

"I've been living down in Kingsport for about half a year." Silas sat and sipped his coffee, the bitter brew scalding a line down his throat.

"Looks like you gained some tattoos and lost an eye on your adventures."

"Lost the eye to a fellow with broken bottle and a temper in Bangkok, and I don't rightly remember where I got all the tattoos."

Martin laughed and grinned again. "And now you're back and you bought this little tub? With your experience, you could captain one of those big trawlers scooping up haddock off Stellwagen Bank and make a fortune!"

"Oh, that's not for me." Silas shook his head with a rueful smile. "I'd rather be my own boss and run my own boat." He patted the cabin side with real affection. "*Sea Change* is a stout little ship. I can hand-line cod and haddock by myself, and run pots year around."

"Lobster?" Martin made a disdainful face. "You'll go broke. Didn't know there were any left!"

"A few if you know where to look." Silas shrugged. "I pick up other jobs, too. I've got a diving rig and do some deep-sea salvage work that pays pretty good."

Martin's face blanched. "You mean you go under*water* in one of them hard-hat contraptions?"

"Sure." Silas grinned at his cousin's reaction. "It's not all that dangerous."

Martin snorted in disgust. "You couldn't pay me enough!"

"Well, I may not get rich, but I don't have anyone but myself to answer to."

"And what brings you up to Arkham in this weather? More work?" Martin looked honestly curious.

"Can't go to sea in this blow, so I took a job from Old Man McIntire to haul a load of lobster pots down to Kingsport in the morning." Silas sighed and wiped the water from his brow. He'd come to Arkham to talk to Martin, but couldn't say that was the main reason he'd come. He had to ease into this. Just like bringing his boat into the dock, these waters were turbulent. "Truth be told, Martin, I wanted to talk to you about some things, too. Part of the reason I came back to New England."

"And what reason's that, besides drivin' all the young ladies to distraction by walkin' around shirtless in the middle of a nor'easter?" Martin laughed at first, but he sobered when Silas didn't respond. "What is it, Silas? What's happened?"

"Nothing's really *happened*, but…" He rubbed his eye and tried to think of how to put it into words. "I went to sea to get away from Innsmouth. You know what the town's like. No place for a kid to grow up. But the sea felt right, too. I always felt better on the ocean, but the last couple of years, I just…"

"Just what?"

"I can't say exactly, Martin." *Not without sounding completely insane.* "You heard my parents passed away, didn't you?"

"Yes. A shame, too. They weren't that old."

"Thanks." He sipped his coffee and searched for words. As usual, he came up short. "After I got the news, I felt this need to come back."

"Well, that's natural."

"I thought so too, at first, but…" He sighed in frustration and blundered on. "Do you ever dream of the sea, Martin?"

"Sometimes." Martin looked perplexed at the sudden change of subject. "Doesn't everyone who's been a sailor?"

"Not like mine." Silas stared down into his coffee. "I have nightmares, Martin. They were just a few at first, and I thought it was guilt for my parents, but now they come every time I sleep. They're so vivid… I dream of the sea, but not like I did when I was a kid, not with the feeling like I wanted to be a sailor."

"How then?" All humor had fled Martin's voice, and his lips were set in a hard line.

"I dream *under* the sea, and I see faces, bloated faces with bulging eyes. They remind me of people I knew as a boy, half-drowned, but not dead." Silas shivered, but not from the chill gusts blowing through the open door. Pointed teeth grinned, webbed hands reaching for him, glowing eyes in the darkness… He couldn't tell Martin those details, of course. Some things you couldn't say aloud if you wanted to stay out of the madhouse. "I wanted to know whether you ever had dreams like that. Dreams of people you knew turned into…something horrible. Voices calling you to join them. We both know the Marsh family's an odd lot. I need to know if this is some family affliction, if I'm going crazy, or if you've ever had any—"

"No." Martin downed his coffee and stood so abruptly his leg jostled the table. "Nope, I never dreamed any such thing, Silas, and you best forget you ever did, too!"

Martin turned for the door and grabbed his slicker, but Silas clutched his arm before he donned it. "Martin, wait! I just want to ask you—"

"Don't ask me anything, Silas." Martin glared at the hand gripping his arm. "I got no answers for you."

Silas didn't release his grip. "You don't have answers, or you just won't *give* me any?"

"I don't *have* any." Martin jerked away and pulled on his slicker. "You want answers to questions like that, you go talk to the main family in Innsmouth. I made my peace with them years ago. I don't bother them, and they don't bother me."

Martin stomped out the door into the weather.

"Martin, wait!" Silas gritted his teeth, then spied his cousin's sou'wester hanging on a peg. He snatched it up and stepped out onto the deck. "Martin, your hat!"

Martin was already up on the quay, but stopped and turned back. Silas stepped up onto the boat's gunnel and held up the hat. When Martin reached down to take it, Silas refused to let go.

"Don't just run off, Martin. You're the last person I can talk to."

"No, I'm not." He jerked the sou'wester out of Silas's hand and put it on, his face set in a hard scowl. "You talk to the old family. Get your answers there. But I'll warn you, Silas, you may not like what they have to tell you. You've been gone a long time, and you know how they feel about strangers, even ones who share their name!" Martin whirled away and strode off down the quay.

Silas stood in the rain glaring at his cousin's receding back. *Answers…why is it always so hard to just get a simple answer?* His cousin knew something about the nightmares that plagued him, but he wouldn't or *couldn't* speak about it. Why? The main family of Marshes harbored many secrets—everyone from Innsmouth knew that—but were they also hiding some hereditary malady of madness or delusion?

Silas suppressed a shiver of revulsion. He'd visited Innsmouth briefly upon his return from abroad, but the pallid faces and watery eyes of his cousins there gave him chills deeper than any nor'easter that ever blew. He'd left without speaking to anyone, feeling as if he'd rather walk into the sea and never return than face the Marshes of Innsmouth.

Better to untie *Sea Change* and head downriver, sail out to sea and never come back. But that wasn't an option. Only a fool went to sea with a nor'easter brewing, and yet, only at sea did he feel at peace. *No wonder people think I'm strange…a sailor who only ever wants to go back to sea.* He looked up into the weeping sky and knew in his bones the weather wouldn't clear for at least three days. Three days sitting on a dock, listening to the siren call of the sea echoing in his head.

"Nothing to do but keep busy," he grumbled, bending to shift some of the deck gear to make room for Old Man McIntire's lobster pots.

As he bent to that task, however, a piercing whistle and call from up the pier drew his attention. *Did Martin change his mind?* But when looked up, what he saw stopped him cold. "What in the name of…"

A woman walked down the quay, but a woman unlike the usual sort seen on the waterfront. Ramrod straight, wearing a gray dress buttoned up tightly from throat to waist, but no coat, she walked with quick, stiff steps that reminded him of a partridge. She clutched a black umbrella in one hand to fend off the rain, and, of all things, a thick book in the other. The latter she held close, as if it could shield her from the three men who had stepped off a barge to block her path.

Silas gritted his teeth. He couldn't hear what they said to her over the hiss of rain, but he didn't have to. Her eyes darted between them as she stopped short, a look of wide-eyed desperation on her face. He knew where this was going. He'd seen this too much in his travels, women accosted and treated like chattel, and not just abroad. Even after the government gave women full suffrage, some men treated them like they should be subservient. The sight of it happening here prickled his skin like a plague of nettles.

Not on my watch... Silas grabbed a slicker from the pilothouse and pulled it on. Men didn't go shirtless in front of ladies, after all. By the time he'd climbed up to the quay, however, the three men were backing away from the woman. One of them turned with a look of unease on his face. The woman took a step toward them, but he couldn't hear what she said.

"Off with you, ya crazy cow!" the largest of the men bellowed, flicking a meaty hand in a shooing motion, although it was he who was retreating from her.

The woman's eyes followed them beseechingly. "Please, I just..." But the men weren't listening, muttering under their breath as they stepped back aboard their barge.

Not knowing what she'd said to send them packing, but admiring her spunk, Silas took a closer look at her. She was younger than he'd guessed from her conservative clothes and severe hairstyle—maybe late twenties or early thirties. Her plain gray dress, speckled black by the rain, looked like something a spinster of sixty might wear. She was slim, straight-backed, with brown hair pulled into a low bun, a few curls escaping to dangle upon her furrowed brow. The book she clutched to her chest was large, thick, and leather bound. Her eyes flicked around, searching, desperate. Her earlier distress hadn't been about being accosted at all. She was looking for something—or someone—and her gaze alighted on him.

Silas turned away, not wanting to look like another ruffian. But a conservatively dressed woman wandering the wharves alone, out in a storm without a coat, clutching a book was nigh strange. Whether she was desperate or mad as a hatter, Silas had no desire to get involved in someone else's problems. As he started to climb back down to *Sea Change*, however, her voice called him back.

"Sir?" She bustled toward him, her birdlike gait closing the distance with surprising speed. "Please, sir, I need the help of a sailor.

Please! The…the end of days is fast approaching, and I don't know where else to find help!"

"The *what?*" *Desperate* and *mad, maybe,* he thought, but he couldn't simply ignore her. His own pleas for help had gone unanswered for too long.

"The end of *days*!" She tottered up, stopping barely a step away, her eyes wide and her knuckles white on the book clutched to her breast. Her lower lip trembled, her weak chin quivering. "All the works of man will fall! The stars…the travelers will come…everything…*everyone* will perish! The tome foretells it all! You have to *help* me!"

"I…" Silas closed his mouth to keep from saying something offensive. He didn't know if she was truly touched in the head or some kind of religious fanatic, but the book she clutched so fervently wasn't a Bible. The tooled leather looked more like some of the things he'd seen in the Far East than anything from a church, and although the woman dressed primly, she didn't talk like a Bible-thumper. *Not your problem, Silas…* "I really can't help you, miss."

The words sounded gut-wrenchingly familiar. *No help…no answers…no one who trusts enough to help.*

"*Please*, sir!" She tilted her umbrella out of the way as she stepped closer, and the nor'easter filled it like a sail, jerking it out of her grasp and flinging it into the river. She didn't even glance after it, but she clutched his arm. "I know this sounds mad, but I need a sailor, someone who knows how to navigate with the stars, to interpret something from this tome." She sheltered the book with her body even as rain soaked her hair. "Lives…no, the very *world* depends on this! Please!"

"The stars?" Not crazy, maybe, but clearly disturbed, she obviously needed help, and having just been refused by his cousin, her desperation struck Silas a blow. *If you turn her away, what kind of hypocrite will you be, Silas?* Perhaps if he could just talk her down a little, she would move on to a safer area of Arkham. Ladies like her didn't belong on the docks. "You mean celestial navigation? You need someone to take a fix from some numbers in that book?"

"Yes! Precisely!" She withdrew her hand and clutched the book closer in a futile attempt to protect it from the rain. "I'm sorry. My name is Abigail Foreman. I'm a librarian at the university. This tome speaks of the end of mankind, a path between stars opening, horrible things entering our world at a very specific time and place. The place is denoted by celestial data, but the time and numbers keep changing."

"Changing?" Now that *did* sound crazy. Books didn't change. But a closer look at the tome's tooled leather cover confirmed that this was no mariner's log, almanac, or explorer's diary.

"*Please*, Mister..."

"Marsh. Silas Marsh." Her plea finally broke his reticence. Crazy or not, maybe if he spoke to her, offered to help, he could calm her down. "You're getting soaked, Miss Foreman. You best step aboard and have a cup of java to warm you while you tell me what you need."

"Oh, *thank* you, Mister Marsh!" She followed him to the edge of the quay, but then peered dubiously down at the deck of the boat. "Are you sure..."

One look at her hard-soled shoes and he knew she'd have a problem stepping onto the gunnel. Doing so without letting go of the book she clutched so dearly would make it perilous. Falling into the raging Miskatonic River would be deadly for someone dressed in heavy skirts.

"Here, miss. I'll help you." Silas stepped down to the pitching gunnel and braced one foot on the quay wall. His stance sure, he held up two hands. "Don't worry."

"Thank you, Mister Marsh." She inched forward and started to step down, both hands still firmly gripping the book.

Her shoe met the rain-slicked cap rail and shot out from under her as if she'd stepped on ice. A clipped cry escaped her lips, but before she fell, Silas's hands closed around her waist and he lifted her down to the deck as easily as plucking a lobster pot from the sea. She wobbled as *Sea Change* rolled, but he was down and gripping her elbow firmly in a flash.

"Here, miss, just step inside and have a seat." Silas guided her into the cabin and waved her to the bench beside the chart table. He hung up his slicker and grabbed a towel from the wet locker. "Sorry for the rough handling. Let me just get a shirt on." He handed the towel over and hurried forward to get a shirt from the fo'c'sle. The thick flannel felt sticky on his wet skin, but he didn't want to offend the poor woman.

When he reentered the cabin, however, he found her drying off the book with the towel, not, as he'd intended, her dripping face and hair. Perhaps librarians cared more for their books than their own condition. He quickly poured her a cup of coffee and put it down on the table.

"Here you go." He topped up his own cup and sat down across from her. "Now, what's this about that book? You said it changed? How can that be?"

"I don't know *how*, Mister Marsh, but the entry *does* change!" Abigail finished dabbing at the rain-specked leather and pressed the towel to her face, then dried her hands meticulously before touching the volume. "This is a book of prophecies written by an excommunicated monk in the sixteenth century. I became interested in this particular prophecy because the date of its occurrence is very near to today's date."

Silas arched an eyebrow. Although the edges of the leather were cracked with age, the book looked remarkably well preserved for being four hundred years old, and he suddenly understood her concern for its condition. The cover was deeply tooled with strange symbols and figures around the foreign title: *Prophesiae Profana*.

"I should never have taken it out of the library, but I needed proof." Abigail sighed and finally noticed the coffee he'd placed before her. She wrapped her hands around the hot metal cup and lifted it to her lips, sipping carefully. "I'm afraid I was rather...distraught when I discovered the date and stellar data had changed. I grabbed the tome and my umbrella and completely forgot to put on a coat!" She fumbled a tiny notebook out of a handbag she held clutched beneath the book. "But look here!"

Abigail pointed to two rows of numbers beside the names of planets and stars. Silas recognized the names of celestial bodies commonly used for navigation, the angles of their sightings from the horizon, and the exact times of the sightings down to the second.

"I jotted this first note down to convert the dates from Julian to Gregorian."

"From what?" Had she slipped into some foreign language?

"The commonly used calendar changed after the tome was printed, so I had to convert it. Then, I took the stellar data to Professor Withers, the university astronomer. He told me he was too busy to help, that there was some strange phenomenon occurring in the heavens that he had to study. He said I should seek out a sailor who knew celestial navigation." She pointed to the second row of data. "When I returned to the library, the date, time, and stellar data had changed to these! I wrote them down immediately, thinking I must have made a mistake, but then realized I couldn't have! There's only one entry in this entire passage, and I couldn't have gotten the information from nowhere! So, I grabbed the book and came down here to find a sailor who could tell me where on Earth these entries point to." She looked up at him. "Can you do that?"

"Yes, but…" Silas didn't want to tell her that two scratched notes in a notebook weren't proof of anything.

"Just let me show you the prophecy. It's in Latin, but I can translate."

Silas clenched his teeth against a sarcastic retort. How convenient that this book was in a language he couldn't read. She could tell him the book said anything she wanted, and he'd be forced to accept her word. Calling her a liar, however, wouldn't do him any good.

As Abigail gingerly opened the tome, Silas found his eyes drawn to the pages, their hand-written block print framed by artistic illustrations that filled the margins. He'd seen books like this before, old texts crafted by monks in distant monasteries, artfully decorated with depictions of holy scenes or relics. She turned the pages carefully, one at a time.

"Please, look here, Mister Marsh." She opened her notebook and put it down beneath the celestial notations in the book. "This passage explains that a door will open to issue forth the hordes of fiends from another place, a hellish place, and those hordes and the…beings that rule them will destroy the world of man and all our works will fall into ruin."

"I'll have to take your word on that, Miss Foreman." He tried not to sound derisive, but the passage could have been a recipe for goulash for all he could tell.

"And these numbers here are…" She pointed to a row of text, but then gasped, "Oh, dear Lord."

"What?"

"Look!" She turned the book so he could see and pointed to the line of stellar names and numerals. Even in Latin, Silas recognized the names of Altair and Jupiter. Then Abigail placed her open notebook flat and pointed. "I recorded that second set just *hours* ago! Now they've changed again! See?"

Silas looked at the notation, then the text, and indeed they were different. The one in the tome itself was only five days hence, but that also didn't prove anything. A simple error or some delusion on Abigail's part could explain the disparity. Books simply didn't change. But as he opened his mouth to reiterate this point, his eye drifted to the illustrations filling the margins of the tome. Cold fingers gripped his heart, twisting his guts into knots. Abigail's voice faded into the roar of rain on the cabin roof as his mind stumbled in disbelief.

Nightmares writhed along the periphery of the pages, twisted limbs, deformed and misshapen faces with bulging eyes and needle teeth like some sort of misbegotten serpents. But it was the faces that most gripped his attention, for Silas had seen them before. He saw them every night when he closed his eyes to sleep.

"Mister Marsh?" Abigail looked at him with concern. "Is there something wrong? You look..."

"Nothing." Silas swallowed half of his cup of coffee, biting back a curse at his burned tongue. He looked away, out the porthole, across the cabin, anywhere as his mind spun. *Impossible. It's a coincidence, some trick or other.* He'd never seen this book before, but images such as these were surely copied from others, and he'd seen a lot of strange inscriptions in the distant ports of Indonesia and the South Pacific. He gulped the rest of his scalding coffee and heaved a sigh to steady his nerves. No, it had to be a coincidence. "Now, about these changes...I don't see how—"

"I assure you, Mister Marsh, I am *not* making this up!"

Silas looked at the data again. "When was this book written?"

"Fifteen forty-one, AD," Abigail said, her voice trembling. "But this piece of text was transcribed from a scroll much older."

Silas looked at her skeptically. "I don't think they had clocks or sextants so accurate that long ago. As for prophecies about the end of the world, I've heard dozens. Every culture has one."

Her lips thinned into a hard line. "I'm *not* crazy, Mister Marsh!"

"I'm not saying you're crazy, Miss Foreman, but think. Books don't just change. There has to be an explanation. Someone must be playing an elaborate trick on you or something."

"How? The tome hasn't left my hands since this afternoon?"

"I don't know, but whoever's doing this isn't as smart as they think!" He tapped her notes, then pointed to the page. "The calculations for celestial navigation are tricky, and working up fixes from nothing would require real expertise. If these are someone's idea of a sick joke, something just to scare you, working out the fixes should show it."

She looked puzzled. "I don't understand."

"Making up numbers like these will more than likely give nonsense results if I do the calculations." He pointed to the data. "See how each fix uses two celestial bodies?"

"Yes."

"Well, if someone made these up as a trick, chances are that these two fixes won't point to any spot on the globe." That certainly made more sense than some moldy old book accurately foretelling the end of the world down to the second, let alone the text changing as if by magic from one hour to the next. "If they *are* made up, I should be able to tell you so."

"Very well, Mister Marsh." Abigail snatched up her notebook and wrote down the third set of numbers, then ripped out the page and handed it to him. "I'll pay you ten dollars to calculate the locations from these celestial fixes or prove them false."

"What?"

"Prove to me this is a hoax!" Abigail rooted through her handbag and came out with a wad of banknotes. She thrust the cash at him. "*Please*, Mister Marsh! I'll sleep better if you do prove this is some sick joke."

"Call me Silas." He pushed the money away and stood, dragging his eyes away from the tome that so accurately depicted his nightmares. "I'll work up the numbers for you, but not today."

"Why ever not?" she asked incredulously.

"Because..." *Because I need a drink!* Silas gestured out the open door at the darkening sky. "The calculations take time, and it's getting late. You should be getting home. I'll walk you. It's not fit for man nor beast out, and some rough types loiter along the waterfront. I'll do the calculations tonight and bring you the results in the morning."

"Um, yes, okay." Abigail stood and wrinkled her nose at the pouring rain out the door. "Oh, fiddlesticks! I lost my umbrella."

"You can wear this." Silas pulled his slicker out of the wet locker and a sou'wester as well. "It'll keep your book drier than an umbrella."

"But you—"

"I'm fine." He helped her into the oversized slicker and hat, then banked the stove and guided her out on deck. "Now let me help you up onto the quay. Falling in the river might not end the world, but it'll end your life right enough."

"You have a way of stating things in matter-of-fact terms, Silas. Thank you." She didn't quibble about rough handling or his hands on her waist when he lifted her up onto the quay as some women would have. "And call me Abigail, please."

"All right, Abigail. Now, let's get a wiggle on before the really rough types come out of their holes." The slashing rain soaked his shirt as he guided her down River Street, but he found the chill strangely comforting after the stuffy cabin and disconcerting prophecy.

Chapter Two

The Miskatonic River

The iron back door of the Golden Plaice clanged closed behind Silas, and the blustery nor'easter slapped him in the face. After his encounter with Abigail Foreman, he'd needed a stiff drink, and two whiskeys had reinforced his long-practiced denial of such hokum. Nightmares, sure, everyone had nightmares, but the notion that some moldy four hundred-year-old tome could predict the end of the world down to the second was rubbish. The illustrations' resemblance to his nightmares had to be simple coincidence. Myths of sea monsters were as common as barnacles on boats, and this was undoubtedly just another sea story. He'd transform Abigail's humbug prophecy into ten clams hard cash, load up Old Man McIntire's lobster pots, and get back to his life.

My life... He hunched his shoulders against the wind and strode down the narrow alley toward River Street, welcoming the chill rain that soaked him to the skin. Abigail had wanted to give him back his coat and hat, but he'd told her to wear them until she could get another umbrella. He'd pick them up from her tomorrow when he gave her the location of her prophetic Armageddon. *Nightmares and monsters and the end of the world... What a crock of bilge water!*

And yet the chill down his spine wasn't entirely due to the rain trickling down his back. Deny as he might, something about this whole thing wasn't quite right. It felt like an itch he couldn't quite scratch. The illustrations had been too familiar. He must have seen them somewhere before, and whatever subtle insanity plagued the Marsh clan had latched onto them. Abigail had said the legend had been copied from an even older scroll. Others may have copied that scroll over the centuries, and those copies could have ended up in museums all over the world. He'd certainly seen a lot of strange things in his travels, and that would explain everything.

Emerging from the narrow alley onto River Street, Silas glanced back the way he'd come with the practiced vigilance of a world traveler. He hadn't been exaggerating when he told Abigail that the waterfront spawned some rough characters, and he'd learned the hard way to watch his back after being shanghaied once in Montevideo. Silas was a big man, his arms and chest well-muscled with years of labor, and although he'd had a couple of drinks, he was far from drunk. If someone jumped him, they'd better be toting iron or they'd be in for a surprise.

Back in the alley, the gleam of light on something silvery caught his eye. A car clattered by on the street, and the light of its headlamps swept into the alley for a moment. A hunch-shouldered figure stood there, its large eyes and a wide mouth illuminated for an instant. Silas blinked, shaking off a shiver of familiarity, and moved on. *Probably just some rum-soaked old sot.* But he hadn't noticed anyone there when he'd left the speakeasy.

Silas crossed River Street, striding east along the quay. He cast another covert glance over his shoulder. The stooped figure stood at the mouth of the alley he'd just left, cloaked in a slicker and hat, collar turned up against the rain, face in shadow. *Following me?* But the man just stood there as if waiting…or watching.

Silas wasn't sure whether his uneasiness was due to his encounter with Abigail, or his usual discomfort with dry land under his boots. He knew well how to cure that uneasiness, however, and shake off any ne'er-do-well trying to stalk him at the same time.

Silas stepped aboard *Sea Change*, slipped her stern line, then ducked into the cabin and stowed his sodden shirt in the wet locker. Feeling better already with the motion of the river under his boots and cool air against his skin, he knelt, opened the engine room hatch, primed the carburetor, and hauled on the crank start. The engine sputtered to life. He closed the hatch and reached over to feel the belly of the stove. It was warm, but not hot, and he'd want coffee. A wad of newspaper, a few sticks of dry kindling, and a match quickly resurrected the flame. While the stove and the engine warmed up, he filled the percolator and secured the pot in the fiddles on the stove, then shoved a few more sticks of wood into the fire.

Ready to go.

Striding up to the pilot house, Silas jammed the shifter into forward and revved the engine up just enough to take the tension off the bow line. He flipped the switch that ignited the boat's electric running lights and stepped out of the pilothouse door. Shielding his eye from the rain, he scanned the river for traffic and found it clear; apparently no one else was crazy enough to be on the water on such a foul night. Glancing up and down the quay, he saw no one. Either his stalker had given up, or he'd been imagining it. A flick unwound the bow line from the piling and he stepped back into the pilothouse. Silas freed up the wheel, eased her to port, and pulled *Sea Change* out into the turbulent waters of the Miskatonic, pointing her bow downriver. Glancing back at the quay again, he saw a few bargemen or longshoremen hurrying this way and that, bent against the rain, but no one watching him. *Just my imagination.*

Silas squinted through the rain-streaked windows into the storm, silently cursing his lost eye. Navigating the Miskatonic in the dark was challenging enough, adding a nor'easter elevated the risk, and doing so without decent depth perception made it even worse. The tide should have slacked by now, but it was still ebbing hard.

Sea Change shot under the Peabody Avenue Bridge like a bullet from a gun. As the lights of Arkham passed astern, his vision improved. Once he cleared the Rivertown bend, and trees lined the shore instead of houses, Silas turned the boat up current and eased her over to the northern shore into a familiar anchorage.

Silas kicked *Sea Change* out of gear and strode up to the bow. The boat immediately drifted downriver, but the release of the brake on the windlass sent seventy pounds of anchor and thirty feet of heavy chain plunging to the bottom. He paid out another couple hundred feet of anchor rode, then secured it. The line came taut and the boat lurched around into the flow.

Silas stood there in the rain awhile, watching the shore to make sure the anchor held. Rain trickled through his hair, down his shoulders and back, washing away his unease, the comforting roll of the deck beneath his boots massaging his soul. The Miskatonic wasn't the sea, but at least he was on the water.

Content that the anchor was set, Silas ducked back into the cabin to the intoxicating scent of percolating coffee. He toweled off, cleaned up the wet floor, lit a kerosene anchor lamp, and shut off the boat's running lights. The engine wheezed to silence as he shut it down, and the blustery howl of the nor'easter settled in. Kicking off his sodden boots and soaked pants, he hung them to drip in the wet locker, wrapped the towel around his waist, and poured himself a cup of java. From the cupboard beneath the table, he liberated a bottle labeled "Medicinal Spiritus Frumenti," and topped off his cup. The scent of Canadian whiskey mingled with that of coffee. The first sip of the heady brew set his teeth on edge, just the tonic he needed to sharpen his mind for the task at hand.

Sitting at the chart table, Silas pulled out his own tomes—*The American Ephemeris and Nautical Almanac for 1926* and the current volume of declination tables. The almanac contained the positions of the sun, moon, planets, and certain stars for every hour of every day of the year, and tables for calculating adjustments down to the second. The declination tables gave him the ability to convert the angles of these sightings, with some laborious calculations, into angular distances from the celestial equator, and thence into latitude and longitude. Each fix had two sightings, which added accuracy by simple triangulation.

For the author of Abigail's prophecy in 1540 to give the stellar data for a position on Earth four hundred years in the future would have been impossible, which was why he didn't expect the calculations to yield anything but gibberish. Silas copied Abigail's data onto a sheet of paper and began the meticulous process that would transform the numbers into latitude and longitude. He was no mathematician, but long practice had made these calculations so familiar that he had little trouble. Still, they were involved, and he found his unease dwindling even further with the occupation of his mind.

Silas's brow furrowed as he finished the first fix. The result actually gave a meaningful location, and somewhere in the northwest Atlantic at that. Well, the accompanying stellar fix would certainly tell the tale. He ran through the calculations and stopped cold. For a moment, he thought he'd run the same fix twice, but when he rechecked, he found that wasn't the case.

Someone's pulling a fast one, he thought, for the two locations he'd calculated weren't just close, they were identical. Nobody took fixes that accurately, even in perfect conditions with modern equipment. This had to be some well-planned hoax. *Well, we'll see just how deep this hoax goes.*

Silas started on the second set of data. The time of the sighting was two days nearer than the first, and the third set was a day closer than that one. He smirked as he ran the numbers. It sure seemed like someone was trying to scare Abigail.

The numbers resolved and again he stared in disbelief. "Well blow me down." The position denoted was exactly the same as the first two, right down to the minute and second of longitude and latitude. He gritted his teeth and ran the next fix, knowing what he'd find. Sure enough, it came up the same.

Now for the ones I watched her copy from the book.

He ran the numbers meticulously, forcing himself to be careful. When they both came up exactly the same as the others, he sat back with a snort of disgust. "Impossible. It's got to be a trick!" But why would anyone try to pull such a trick on a librarian?

The position was somewhere near New England, north of Boston. Working up all the numbers from different times and sightings would have been a monumental task, and if someone were really trying to scare her, the location would have been someplace she knew, like her apartment or the library. He remembered her mentioning an astronomer at the university, but couldn't think of any reason why someone like that would want to scare a librarian?

There was only one more thing to do: find that location on a chart.

Downing his whiskey-spiked coffee and putting the cup aside, Silas rifled through his store of charts beneath the table's hinged top. He chose two, one that displayed the coast from Boston to Cape Ann, and another from the Cape to the Merrimack River. Laying them flat and checking the latitude of his calculation, he knew instantly the spot would be north of Cape Ann. He picked a pair of dividers and parallel rulers from the rack of tools.

"Forty-two, forty-two, point oh three..." He walked off the latitude on the chart's sidebar and drew a line with his ruler. "Zero seven zero, forty-five, point nine." Another line marked the longitude, and they crossed just east of the mouth of Plum Island Sound and the town of Innsmouth.

Silas dropped his pencil, coffee roiling in his stomach. "Devil Reef."

He knew those waters well, having fished them in his youth. They were some of the best fishing grounds north of Cape Ann, and the main Marsh family did not suffer outsiders plying those waters. He'd heard stories aplenty about that reef, from ghost ships wrecked there in centuries past, to more recent reports during the war of strange lights beneath the water, and even figures dancing on the exposed reef at low tide when the moon was new.

Sailors were a superstitious lot, and Silas had heard tales of ghosts and haunts from Singapore to Maine, but the locals of Innsmouth believed the tales about Devil Reef. He had always considered the stories nothing but superstitious drivel contrived to keep strangers away, but all the same, he took heed. Silas fished his old logbook from under the table and started flipping pages, looking for his notes on Devil Reef.

But why would someone concoct such an elaborate hoax to fool a librarian into thinking the end of the world was going to take place there?

Something thumped hard against the hull, and *Sea Change* lurched on her anchor, snapping Silas out of his musing. He was up in a heartbeat, dropping his logbook and reaching for his powerful electric lamp. *The last thing I need is a floating stump to foul the anchor line or damage the rudder!* Pulling on his sodden pants, he turned down the cabin lamp so the light wouldn't ruin his view outside, and stepped out into the storm.

Silas shone his light over each side and the stern but saw only turbid brown water. He went forward through the cabin and out the pilothouse door, checked the anchor line, and found it tight. Shielding his eye from the slashing rain and peering into the gloom, he noted that the few lights on the far shore weren't changing position. *At least the anchor's not dragging.* He relaxed a little. *Sea Change* wagged back and forth as the wind and current fought for control over the small boat, but the impact of something heavy hitting the hull had been unmistakable. Flotsam floated past: tree limbs, trash, even an old boot, but nothing large enough to cause that kind of lurch.

Must have been a log or something, he resolved, squinting into the distance looking for larger floating debris. Something silvery flashed beneath the surface, a roil of water, then nothing. *Sea Change* lurched again, swinging hard on her anchor, but this time there was no thump against the hull.

Just the current and wind playing hay with her now, he concluded, but something had hit the boat before. "Anchoring out in the river in a nor'easter, Silas? You're lucky you weren't hit by a barge broken loose!" The tide still seemed to be ebbing harder than it should. With this rain, the river would continue to run, but the shift of tide should have eased the flow by now. He had no option but to ride it out, as motoring back upriver to town and docking in the dark would be more dangerous than staying put. He scanned the dark river once again but saw nothing.

Ducking back through the pilothouse to the main cabin, thinking of another whiskey-laced coffee, Silas reached up for the overhead lamp but then froze. His chart, logbook, the papers with his calculations, and the notes from Abigail were gone, and there was water all over the table.

"Who the hell..." He whirled to shine his light down into the fo'c'sle, but there was nobody there. He'd just come through the pilothouse, and there was no place to hide there either. He turned back to direct the light out the aft door onto the deck. The cabin floor was wet. He'd walked through from the aft deck, and his wet footprints were clear, but there was a second set beside his that went to the chart table, then forward to the engine compartment hatch.

Somebody came aboard, but there's no other boat out here. Silas would have seen one when he was on the bow. *How could anyone have gotten aboard?* Then he realized the more pressing question: *And are they* still *aboard?*

Silas stepped to the cabinet opposite the wet locker and pulled out the heavy knife he kept there, pausing to consider grabbing the double-barreled Remington secured to the bulkhead inside. *Best not,* he thought. He had to explore below and needed one hand to carry the lantern. Besides, firing a shotgun aboard a boat below the waterline was a great way to blow a hole in the hull. No, for the engine compartment and the fo'c'sle, the knife was better.

Working his way forward, shining his light on the deck, he saw that the wet footprints were larger than his own and splayed wide at the toe. They stopped at the engine compartment hatch, but he couldn't tell if they went back out the aft door. Someone standing there could see through the pilothouse windows to the foredeck, and they might have stood here watching him. Suppressing the urge to call out in an attempt to scare the intruder off, he slipped the knife through his belt and bent to grip the handle of the engine room hatch. Taking a deep breath, he jerked the hatch open and shone his light down into the compartment.

Nothing but a wave of heat and a greasy old engine greeted him. A quick visual check revealed no intruder, no wet footprints, and nothing obviously tampered with, so he closed the compartment and continued his search. There were no more wet footprints forward except his own, but he checked the pilothouse and the fo'c'sle as well. Finding nothing out of place, and no more signs anyone had been there, he returned to the main cabin. The water on the table and missing papers confirmed that this wasn't some hallucination induced by bad hooch, but who would steal a bunch of papers?

"And how the hell did you get aboard?"

Silas went back over his departure from the Arkham quay in his mind. Could someone have gotten aboard and hidden someplace while he started the engine? It was possible someone could have leapt from the quay to the cabin roof, although he would have heard the thump or felt the boat lurch. He looked up, as if he could see through the cabin roof. Could they have climbed back up there?

Now's the time for some firepower. He traded his knife for the Remington, checked the loads, and worked out how to hold both the gun and the lamp. He shone the light across the aft deck from the door, saw nothing, then readied the shotgun and backed out with the twin barrels aimed up at the roof. The powerful lamp shone over the edge of the roof, but there was nothing up there but the stays securing the mast, the overhead boom, the stove's smokestack trailing a streamer of wood smoke, and sheets of slashing rain. Lastly, he checked the fish hold, but that, too, was empty. He scanned the river once again. Even if the intruder had stowed away somehow, they couldn't have gotten away. He would have heard another boat, even with the howling wind. That left only one possibility: someone had slipped over the side to *swim* away, fighting the current, the rain, and the storm.

"Crazy..."

Back inside the cabin, Silas wiped the Remington down with an oilcloth, secured it, and bolted the aft cabin door. He secured the pilothouse door as well, then turned up the cabin lamp and put away his electric light. After toweling dry, he wiped up the water on the cabin sole and table as well, stowing his books and tools. Lastly, he checked the anchor lamp to make sure it had enough kerosene, then took his lantern and the heavy knife forward to the fo'c'sle and lay down in his bunk. Turning down the lamp, he settled in, listening to the howling wind and the burble of water flowing past the hull. The haft of the heavy knife in his hand felt solid and comforting.

No more bumps or unusual lurches rocked *Sea Change*, just the roll of the boat swaying on her anchor, and the mournful moan of the strengthening nor'easter overhead. For Silas, this was as soothing as any lullaby, and he soon found his tension easing and his eyes drooping closed.

As sleep took him, however, nightmare faces loomed out of the darkness, bulbous eyes and wide mouths grinning with needle teeth, but he didn't know if he was dreaming or being plagued by visions of the illustrations in Abigail Foreman's book.

Chapter Three

The Orne Library

Silas stepped up onto the Arkham quay feeling a strange sense of deja vu; the nor'easter still roared, the river still ran like a mill-race, *Sea Change* was docked in exactly the same spot, and he was again going to talk with Abigail Foreman. If not for the fact that his chart, logbook, and Abigail's notes were still missing, he might have convinced himself that he'd dreamed yesterday's odd events.

He crossed River Street and started for the university, splashing through the rain-soaked streets. One block up, he turned onto Main Street and started west. There weren't many people out, and those who were shot him curious looks from under umbrellas or hunkered in raincoats. The damp didn't bother him, long used to working days at sea soaked to the bone, but city folk probably thought he was daft.

Abigail had told him to ask for her at the main information desk of Orne Library. Silas had been to the library only once before and didn't relish visiting again. The librarians hadn't been very friendly. Maybe they'd be less prickly this time since he was just there to see Abigail, not touch any of their priceless treasures. What would Abigail's reaction be when he told her someone had stolen his charts, pages of calculations, logbook, and her notes.

Would she even believe him? Regardless, she would positively flip her lid when he told her all three sets of celestial fixes had pointed to the same spot.

Turning up Garrison Street, he headed south until he reached the university, then crossed and hurried along Church Street. Orne Library hove out of the sheets of rain like a pillared steamship out of a winter squall. Silas crossed the street and dashed up the stone library stairs. When he hauled on the lofty door, it creaked abominably. He wondered if he should tell them to oil the hinges, but decided they probably wouldn't appreciate the advice of a sailor.

The wind grabbed the door when he released it, slamming it shut hard enough to echo through the entry hall and draw a few shocked looks from the patrons in view. Silas shrugged, stomped the water from his boots, shook it from his hair, and promptly sneezed. The air in here felt stuffy and smelled of old paper.

"Shhhh!" A skinny fellow in a black jacket and bow tie glared at him.

"Sorry." Silas wiped his face with his sleeve and asked, "Can you point me to the information desk?"

The man wrinkled his nose and pointed to the centrally located pair of double doors. "It is the desk with the sign that reads 'Information,'" he said in a hushed voice.

"Thank you." Silas ignored the man's snide look, wondering why people whispered the same in churches and libraries.

The huge vaulted room beyond the doors sported three different desks, each with its own polished brass placard: Reference, Lending, and Information. *Probably could have figured that out yourself, Silas,* he thought, altering course to approach the information desk.

Eyes followed his progress across the marble floor. Those of the patrons ranged from curious to surprised, while the librarians looked mildly horrified. The woman at the information desk paled as he approached, stiffened, and licked her lips. Silas tried to smile amiably, but a near-sleepless night filled with nightmares and thoughts of intruders hadn't put him in a pleasant frame of mind.

"Can I help you?" the librarian asked when he was still several steps away.

"I hope so. I'm here to see Abigail Foreman."

"She works in the restricted section." The librarian's eyes traversed him head to foot. "You are *soaking* wet, sir!"

Silas bit back a surly comment. *More flies with honey...* "Yes, I know. I forgot my coat and it's raining out. Could you point me to the restricted section, please?"

"No." She didn't elaborate.

He blinked at her. "Um...why not?"

"Because, sir, it is *restricted*! That means only university faculty and library staff may enter."

"Oh, well, that makes sense, I suppose." Silas reinforced his effort to be civil in the face of rudeness, knowing belligerence would get him nowhere. A legitimate explanation for his presence might serve better. "Could you please have someone fetch Miss Foreman for me, then? She asked me to work out some celestial navigation problems for her, and I have."

"Celestial navigation problems?" she asked dubiously.

"Yes. Sailors use the stars to navigate, you see, and she asked me to—"

"I *know* what celestial navigation is!" she huffed.

"Oh, well, good. Miss Foreman said the astronomy professor was too busy to help her, so you understand why she needed a *sailor* to help her with the calculations." Silas waited for a count of ten, but she just stared at him as if unable to make sense from his words. "So, if you could *please* send someone to fetch Miss Foreman for me, I'll talk to her and stop dripping on your nice polished floor."

She pursed her lips so hard they blanched white. "Very well. Stay here."

She reached under her desk and the high-pitched chime of a bell rang through the chamber. A harried-looking young man in a white shirt and pleated pants emerged from behind the lofty shelves of books.

"Yes, ma'am?"

"Go to the restricted section and tell Miss Foreman that a... man is—"

"Silas Marsh, ma'am," Silas offered.

The librarian flashed him a cold glance. "That a *man* is here to see her."

"Yes, ma'am." The young man hurried off.

Silas kept his face neutral. He understood the librarian's animosity—an unwashed oaf had invaded the halls of higher learning and might damage their priceless works of literature—but that didn't mean he had to like it. Of course, he'd seen enough prejudice against landlubbers from sailors, so such things were a two-way street. He folded his arms and stood there dripping on their floor while he waited.

Finally, Abigail bustled into the room, her short quail steps click-clicking on the floor. Again, she held the tome close to her chest, and her face was alight with something that might have been eagerness mixed with fear. Silas knew that feeling well.

Abigail glanced at the librarian behind the information desk. "Thank you, Evelyn."

"See that your…associate does not damage anything, Abigail. He is *dripping* wet."

Silas opened his mouth to say something, but Abigail beat him to it.

"Mister Marsh is a *sailor*, Evelyn, not a barbarian. He knows the value of books."

The librarian looked skeptical but didn't respond.

"Please, Mister Marsh, let's find someplace quiet to compare our findings."

Any quieter and you could hear a pin drop, he thought, following her as she tap-tapped down an aisle between two towering shelves and through an archway into a smaller chamber. Here, several reading tables and chairs were arranged amid more shelves of books.

"They've changed again!" she hissed in a library whisper as she put her book down on the nearest table. Flipping to the correct page, she pointed to the celestial notations. "Compare them to the ones I gave you!"

"I can't. I don't have them anymore." He leaned near the book and noted that the date and time, at least, were different than those she'd given him the night before. Someone must have changed them again.

"You don't *have* them?" She blinked up at him as if he'd slapped her. "Whatever happened to them?"

"They were stolen off my boat last night while I was anchored out in the river. I don't know who could have done it, or why, but someone stowed away aboard, took your notes, my calculations, logbook, *and* my chart, and *swam* away."

"What?" Her eyes widened and her cheeks paled. "They *swam* the river? Who on Earth would do that?"

"I don't know, but I'll bet you double or nothing on that ten clams you owe me that if I ran the same calculations on *those* numbers," he stabbed a finger at her book, "I'd get the—" Silas stopped cold, staring at the date and time noted in plain block script on the tome's pages. They weren't the same ones he'd seen only moments before. "Abigail..." His finger shook as he pointed to the new numbers.

"What?" She looked and caught her breath, stumbling back a step. She fumbled frantically for her notebook and opened the page, her eyes darting back and forth between the two. "Again! They've changed again!"

"They did! Just this moment!" The chill in his spine turned to ice. Silas had seen a lot of strange things, but never a book that changed letters and numbers by itself. "What in the name of heaven and hell *is* that thing, some kind of hocus pocus?"

"I *told* you they changed! Didn't you *believe* me?" The last came out accusingly.

"I believe you now, sister, and I don't want any part of it." Silas turned away, intending to walk right out of the library, Arkham, and maybe right down to Boston to sign on with the first foreign-bound ship to set sail.

"Wait!" Abigail grasped his arm, her small fingers barely getting a grip on his tense bicep. "You *can't* just leave!"

"The *hell* I can't!" He wrapped his much larger hand around her wrist and pulled her grasping fingers free with little effort. "I'm a sailor, not some kind of magician. I'll have no truck with nonsense like this!"

He turned to go, but she dodged in front of him, her face livid. "You *can't* just go, Silas! You haven't told me what you found! What these numbers mean!"

He stopped and considered shoving past her, but he *had* promised to tell her what he found out. "Fine. All three sets of numbers you gave me pointed to the exact same location. A spot just east of

Innsmouth called Devil Reef."

"Innsmouth..." Abigail glanced past him at the book open on the table, blinked, and bit her lip. She trembled, and blood welled from between her teeth.

"Abigail!" He grasped her arms as tears filled her eyes. "Abigail, stop!"

She drew a ragged breath and her eyes flicked up to his. "Silas... please...look at the numbers again now and tell me I'm not insane."

He let go of her and whirled around to stare down at the tome. Yet again the date, time, and celestial data were different from what they'd been only seconds before. Cold fingers closed around his heart. "Jesus, oh Jesus..."

"It *knows*," Abigail whispered, stepping around him to stare down at the book. "It changes every time I get closer to an answer. First, when I spoke with Professor Withers, then when I spoke with you. It happened again this morning just before you arrived, and now again when you told me the location. Every time I get closer, the answer changes!"

"The time changes, but not the place!" Silas gritted his teeth against the urge to flee, to run away from this intangible threat. "And if you're insane, then so am I, but how can a *book* know anything? How can it *change* anything?"

"I don't know, Silas, but it's the only answer."

"Well, the *book* didn't swim out to the middle of the river last night and climb aboard my boat to steal my chart!" he countered. "Someone left wet footprints across the cabin. Who would...no, who *could* do that? Nobody could swim the Miskatonic the way it's flowing now and survive!"

"No one?" She blinked up at him, then tapped the margin of the tome where fish-like faces stared up from the page with lurid eyes. "No one *human*, you mean."

"No!" Silas stepped back, denial rising like an inexorable tide from his gut. "Those are just pictures, Abigail! They aren't real! They *can't* be..." Silas swallowed hard as his nightmares surged up from his memory, the voices calling him to the sea... *Can there really be a connection to my nightmares?* "Why me, Abigail? Why did you come to *me*?"

"I...I didn't. Well, not you in particular. I was just looking for someone who knew how to navigate using the stars. The other men I spoke with thought I was crazy. Then you seemed to understand." She shook her head. "I thought you believed me."

"I believe you, Abigail. How can I not when I saw it change with my own eyes! But what do you want me to *do* about it?"

"I thought..." She bit her lip again and winced, licking away the blood. Flipping to the page beyond the prophecy, she pointed to a full-page illustration. "I thought you would help me try to stop this. It's Armageddon, Silas! The end of the world!"

Silas's eyes fell on a scene straight out of his nightmares. A vast city beneath the sea loomed up from the page. A huge beast, its wingspan blotting out the sky, rose above masses of shapes. Some were human; others half-fish, half-man; others unnameable horrors; and all were devouring and being devoured in grisly detail.

No one would call Silas Marsh a coward. He'd stared down the throat of a hurricane at sea, sailed the iceberg-strewn Southern Ocean, stood against pirates and cutthroats the world over, but this... The illustration was too much like his visions to be a coincidence.

"Bloody mother of..." Silas clenched his gnarled hands into fists and closed his eye tight, but the half-fish, half-man faces waited there in the darkness for him, calling him home. *Why... Why me? Why do my nightmares and some ancient book foretell the same thing?*

"Silas?"

He snapped his eye open and whirled to face Abigail, gritting his teeth so tightly he thought they might shatter. "Fine! I'll *help* you, but there's not a whole hell of a lot we can do as far as I can see."

"What do you mean?" She still looked scared but wasn't trembling quite so much.

Though loath to touch the vile tome, he flipped back a page and jabbed his finger at the recently transformed entry. "I'll run the calculations on those numbers for you, but if they point to Devil Reef like the others, there's nothing we can do." He tapped a finger on the date and time. "That's only three days away, and this nor'easter's not going to let up before then. I can't take *Sea Change* around Cape Ann in this weather."

"Then they'll win, Silas." Her voice came out as lifeless and cold as a corpse, defeated. "Whatever *they* are, they know we've discovered their plans, and they've changed them to beat us. There's *got* to be an intelligence behind this!"

"They..." Silas furrowed his brow. *These things can't be real. They have to just be nightmares.* Half-man, half-fish—twisted limbs, voices calling to him, calling him home. *Home...* He glared at the margin of the tome and thought of his childhood home, of Innsmouth. *Maybe...maybe the old stories about Devil Reef aren't just stories. And maybe there is a way to get out there and stop this... thing from happening.*

"Maybe..." Silas turned to Abigail and gripped her gently by the shoulders. "Do you have a car?"

"No," she said, but her eyes brightened. "But I can borrow one! Where are we going?"

"We're going to Innsmouth, Abigail." Silas dragged the musty air of Orne Library into his lungs and let it out slowly. Try as he might to avoid the place, the town of his birth seemed to be inexorably drawing him back. "From there, the waters out to Devil Reef are protected from the storm. Someone there might have a boat we can use."

Chapter Four

Innsmouth

The old rattletrap Abigail borrowed had nearly pounded Silas's backside to jelly by the time they crossed the last bridge to Innsmouth. The road from Arkham to Bolton, rough in the best of conditions, had been reduced to a mire of puddles and potholes strewn with debris by the storm. Twice they'd had to stop for Silas to move downed tree limbs from their path. Thankfully, Abigail drove. Silas could pilot a ship through the eye of a needle, but he was all thumbs when it came to cars. Once on the highway, they made better time, although the old flivver could barely make twenty miles in an hour on the best of roads. They stopped in Ipswich for a quick bowl of chowder and a sandwich, and rolled into Innsmouth early that afternoon.

The dilapidated town of Silas's birth greeted them like a stranger in a speakeasy. Pale faces watched from behind rain-streaked windows, and passersby scowled from under broad sou'wester hats. Many buildings had been boarded shut, left vacant after the plague some eighty years ago. Their windows glared like eyes stitched closed, the paint on their clapboard siding peeling with neglect. That nobody ever moved into those empty houses from other towns seemed normal to Silas when he was growing up here. Now, he wondered why.

"Looks like the place has seen better days," Abigail said as they clattered up Eliot Street and rounded the old statue in the square. Turning onto State Street, they paralleled the roaring Manuxet River until, finally, he caught a glimpse of the ocean ahead.

"It has." Silas struggled to keep his voice even. There had been little cheer for a young boy to find in a town like this, and the only time he'd regretted leaving had been when he received news that his parents had died. "Good-sized ships used to run cargo in and out of here back in the day, but storms silted in the harbor. There was talk of dredging, but the only folks in town who had the money to do it were the Marshes, and they refused to pay. Now only fishing boats come and go, and the old Marsh family has the corner on that market."

"Marsh? Relatives of yours?"

"Yes." Silas didn't elaborate. He hadn't told Abigail his connection with Innsmouth or anything about the old family of Marshes. He'd also kept his nightmares to himself. She'd think him stark raving mad if he told her his dreams were mirrored by the illustrations in her book. But insanity might be a kinder fate than discovering any truth to the tome's prophecy. "I grew up here."

"Well, that's ducky! I mean, your relatives will help us, right?" She stopped at the corner of Water Street and looked at him when he didn't answer. "Right?"

Silas stared out the windshield. From here he could see beyond the spit of land that protected the harbor, beyond the lighthouse flashing across the stormy sky, out the channel with its dented red and green buoys bobbing in the buffeting winds and chop, to the sea. The waves crashing on the rocks called to him, as they always had, but now, instead of the freedom of the sea in their roar, a more sinister susurration urged him. *Come home...* The yearning to heed that call plagued him like a toothache, impossible to ignore.

"Silas?"

Silas tore his gaze from the sea. "Maybe. We'll just have to see." He tamped down the nagging, pleading call echoing with the pounding waves, and pointed left. "Cross the bridge and find a spot on the shore side to park this jalopy. We'll see who we can find to talk to."

"Okay."

Along the shore, the town had fallen into even deeper disrepair.

The old shipping warehouses stood like emaciated scarecrows, weathered down to their bones by years of neglect. Roofs sagged and boards had been stolen from some, while others had completely fallen in, victims of fire, salvagers, or simple vandalism. At the north end of the bay, a dozen or so fishing boats bobbed on moorings near the one remaining fish plant in town, Marsh Seafood.

That, Silas resolved, *will be the last place we'll ask for help.* With any luck, they could find a weathered-in fisherman willing to earn a few bucks and keep his mouth shut. They'd get no help from the main family of Marshes.

The sheltered harbor wasn't much better off than the rundown buildings lining the shore, with half-sunk vessels dotting the once-bustling waterway. The silting had made the harbor unnavigable to all but shallow-draft boats about the size of *Sea Change*. He scanned the water, looking for anything they might rent or borrow. An old ferry sat at one pier, unable to move, stripped of what little brightwork or gear that could be sold. Other large vessels lay scattered about like tombstones in an ill-kept graveyard. There were several relics of the war waiting to be scrapped, and one old cod schooner now down at the stern, her once proud masts denuded and warped. The shipyard itself had fallen into ruin and rust, the jitneys streaked with the hue of dried blood, and powerful cranes thrust up like the bones of a skeleton's rotting fingers reaching from the grave. Smoke streamed away from only one of the old furnace's stacks, the one that the Marshes used for whatever ironwork they still did.

This place, that unforgiving shore, the familiar desolation and ruin, drove the siren song of the waves home within him. *Come to us…come to us…come home…* He felt guilty, that was all. Silas had fled Innsmouth barely out of boyhood, unwilling to be pulled down into decay and neglect with the rest of his relatives. Only his mother had pleaded with him to stay, but he'd refused, thinking a life on the sea would fulfill something in him that Innsmouth never could. He'd always longed for the sea, swimming and fishing as a boy, watching the ships ply the waves. The sea meant freedom, and he'd had that freedom for more than two decades.

And now I'm back… Funny how time makes liars of everyone.

"Where?" Abigail asked, dredging him out of his hypnosis.

"There." Silas pointed to a barn-like structure with an old flatbed truck parked out front. Smoke whipped away from the building's single metal stovepipe, so he knew someone was working. "That's a net loft. There'll be someone there we can talk to." The real question was, would they listen?

"Sure." Abigail pulled over, set the brake, killed the engine, and reached for her newly purchased umbrella.

"It's probably best to let me do the talking here, Abigail." Silas gave her an imploring look. "Folks around here are standoffish. If we start telling them about books that change and prophecies of the end of the world, we won't get anything but blank stares."

"All right." She didn't look happy about it but nodded. "What *are* you going to tell them?"

"I've been working on that." He shrugged and reached for the door handle. "Just follow my lead."

"Okay by me." She opened her door and stepped out under her umbrella.

A quick splash through the rain, and Silas stepped inside the open loft door. Rain drummed on the roof, echoing hollowly within. The air hung thick with pipe smoke, the faint reek of fish, and the acrid tang of burnt coffee. Mounded nets, crates, buoys, coils of line, and various fishing gear littered the loft's periphery so thickly one could barely see the walls. In the center of the cluttered space, wide-mesh gillnets hung from block and tackle overhead. Four men sat on crates there, net needles darting in and out of the mesh, wielded deftly in their thick, calloused hands.

"Afternoon." Silas's greeting drew disinterested glances from three of the men, grizzled old faces beaten into lines of gray by lifetimes on the sea. The fourth, younger, with a wide, pallid face and sloping brow beneath his stocking cap, inspected first Silas, then Abigail with large watery eyes.

Definitely a Marsh. Silas considered turning on his heel and trying to find someone else to talk to, but stood his ground.

"Not the day for an outing to the shore." The young man turned back to his work, his short, spindly fingers handling the mesh with precision.

"That's the truth," Silas admitted, knowing that he and Abigail made an odd pair. He'd worked out a story during the bone-jarring drive that he hoped would sound tempting. "We drove up from Arkham. The lady here works for the university and needs to do some research out on the reef." *True enough, after a fashion.*

"The reef?" The younger man looked up at them again. "What reef?"

"Devil Reef. I'd take her myself, but my boat's in Kingsport, and I can't round Cape Ann in this blow. I'd hoped to rent a boat here."

The man stood and picked up an empty tin coffee cup. "What do you know of Devil Reef?" He strode to the stove and poured liquid as black as tar from the pot.

"I've fished there many times," Silas said with a casual shrug. "I grew up here. My name's Silas Marsh."

The coffee pot clanked down hard on the stove. All four men looked at him, the youngest with his sloped brow furrowed.

"Silas *Marsh*?" one of the older fellows asked around his pipe. "Knew yer father. You left some years back to go a sailin', didn't you?"

"That's right. Saw a good part of the world and put enough aside to buy my own boat. I'm working out of Kingsport now."

"Why the rush to go out?" the young one asked, taking his tin cup back to his crate. "The reef's not going anywhere. Why not wait until this storm blows over?"

"We can't." Abigail stepped up beside Silas, clutching her umbrella in both hands. "There's no time."

"Her project's got a deadline," Silas added, trying to sound casual. "All we need is a boat for a few hours. It's all protected waters from here to the reef."

"I'll pay," Abigail offered. "Ten dollars."

That raised some eyebrows. Ten dollars was more than a day's earnings for the average fisherman.

"*Tch*!" With a scornful look, the young man sat back down and picked up his net needle. "Ten dollars won't buy a new boat. It's too risky. Come back when the weather's laid down."

Silas opened his mouth, but Abigail stepped forward. "We *can't* wait! The time will be passed by then! We have to go *now*!"

"Nobody's goin' out to Devil Reef today, missy."

The gravelly voice from the back of the loft caught Silas by surprise. He peered through the clutter of nets, buoys, rope, and rigging to see two figures, a stooped old woman and a taller man behind her, picking their way forward. There was a small room in the corner, buried in junk, that he hadn't noticed before. The voice had been the old woman's, her stringy gray hair and bent posture telling her years. A gnarled stick in her hand, its wood so black it looked like polished obsidian, thumped the floor with each step. Large, rheumy eyes regarded Silas from under a sloped brow, and her wide, thick lips stretched in a disagreeable frown. Her broad-shouldered companion loomed over her protectively, a man so similar to her in features that they had to be kin. Silas knew that look all too well.

"You're a Marsh," he said, a statement, not a question. "One of the main family."

"I am," she said, rapping her stick on the wooden floor as she tottered up to him. "And nobody goes out to Devil Reef without the approval of Old Man Marsh, which you haven't got."

The three older men continued their work without looking up, but the younger now stood as well. The two Marsh men had rigging knives at their belts, and their intimidating glares might have given a lesser man pause, but Silas remained unimpressed. They wouldn't resort to violence, not against him. However, the old woman's gnarled walking stick—*black coral, not wood,* he noted—made his skin crawl. It seemed to change shape under her knobby knuckles even as he watched.

"And how do we get his approval?" Abigail asked, as dauntless—or clueless—as ever.

The old woman's bulging eyes turned to Abigail, thick lids flicking in a reptilian blink. "You *don't,* missy." She looked to Silas and rapped her stick again, and a chill seeped up through the soles of his boots into his bones. "*He* may be a Marsh, by name if little else, but *you're* not."

"What's going to happen out there?" Abigail blurted. "*Something* is going to happen!"

"Go back to your books, child. There's *nothing* for you here." The old woman rapped the floor twice more with her stick, and her thick lips parted to reveal rows of jagged teeth.

Abigail drew a sharp breath and stepped unsteadily back.

Silas grasped her arm. "Come on, Abigail. Let's go." He clenched his jaw to keep his voice steady and faced down the old woman's smile with the last sour dregs of his courage. "There's no help for us here."

Abigail let him usher her back to the car. She forgot to open her umbrella, and the rain drenched her before he settled her in her seat and closed the door. He cranked the car over and got in the passenger side to find her gripping the wheel in white-knuckled fists.

"What in the name of—" Abigail's voice quavered like a loose shutter in the wind.

"Just drive." Silas glanced back at the open door to the sail loft. The old woman stood there staring at them, the two Marsh men looming at her shoulders. "Just turn around and drive."

"Yes!" Abigail ground gears and wrenched the wheel hard to the left. They lurched around with astonishing speed, as if the car itself longed to be out of this place.

Silas couldn't disagree. He glanced back to see the Marshes still staring at them from the net loft door, watery eyes, pallid faces, wide mouths… *What was I thinking to come back here?*

"Now tell me what the…heck just happened!"

"I'll explain." He pointed straight as they rumbled over the bridge "Drive straight along Water Street until we're out of town, then find a place to pull off. You can see Devil Reef from the beach."

"Fine."

They bounced along the shore road for a quarter mile. To their left, the raging nor'easter broke hard on the rocks until finally the riprap gave way to a wide, sandy beach. Silas gestured to a turnout, and Abigail pulled the jalopy over.

Setting the brake, she turned to face him. "Now what—"

"The old Marsh family's jealous of their fishing grounds. They don't like strangers out there." Silas opened his door and stepped out into the rain, breathing the salty mist in greedy gulps as he stared out over the beach. Breakers curled onto the sloped sand here, their beauty, grace, and power the embodiment of the sea.

"It has *got* to be more than that!" Abigail joined him, gripping her umbrella fiercely against the greedy wind. "That woman…her *face*."

"That's the Marsh family look. The main family, anyway." Silas clenched his hands and let the cool rain wash away his anxiety. "There are stories…about them, and about Devil Reef. I don't know how much of it is true and how much is just made up to run off strangers. I'm only third cousin to the main family. They run the only fish processing plant in town, and pretty much call the shots. They came into real money somehow, more than just from fishing, and they own damn near every going concern in town. They've been known to run off other fishermen who set nets or longlines along the coast hereabouts. That old woman's one of the main family." Silas strode down the rocky incline to the beach, the crunch-squeak of the sand beneath his boots stirring memories from his childhood.

"But she..." Abigail teetered after him in her impractical shoes. "She seemed to *know* why we're here! And why is she so protective of Devil Reef?"

"That's it." Silas pointed across the waves, through the mist-laden air to a thick line of white just below the horizon. "That's Devil Reef, about two miles out. It protects the approach to Innsmouth from the ocean swells, so there's no danger taking a boat out from town. But no sensible captain would round Cape Ann in this weather, and she knows it. All she had to do was say no boat would leave the harbor, and we were done here. No Innsmouth fisherman will flout the Marshes, not if they ever want to sell their catch again."

"But...how...why..."

Silas let the roar of the surf drown out Abigail's questions. It didn't matter any longer, but she wouldn't listen to reason. The crashing waves thrummed up through his legs, their rhythm syncopating with the beat of his heart.

"I swam here as a boy."

Come home...

Silas breathed in the mist like a tonic, taking in the tremulous roar like music, letting it infuse him. "I would swim for hours, just to feel the water."

Come...

"They're my best memories...being in the sea...feeling the waves."

Abigail's voice yammered on behind him, but it was of no more import than the squawking of seabirds.

Be with us...your time is nigh...

Sand squeaked beneath his boots. *Yes... Now... Finally...*

A gull screeched—or was it a voice?—but Silas ignored it. Coolness enveloped his feet, his legs, refreshing...welcoming.

Come home...

Something tugged at his arm, tearing at his shirt, but he pulled away. *The sea...it's all that matters...it's the only thing that will endure…forever.*

Pain lanced through his back as something sharp poked him.

Silas whirled, flinging out a hand to fend off the attack. He snatched the tip of Abigail's umbrella and stared at her in shock.

"Silas!" Her eyes widened and focused past his shoulder. She released her umbrella, turned and ran as well as she could, slogging through knee-deep surf in her sodden dress.

"What the hell?" Silas looked down. He stood thigh deep in the ocean, with no recollection of having waded in. A bone-jarring roar rose behind him.

Silas ducked into the massive curling wave, but the power of the sea was not to be so easily thwarted. It flung him down like a rag doll, smashing him into the hard sand. He went limp, knowing better than to fight that power.

Come to us! The call tore through him with the cool embrace of the sea, a vision of welcoming arms, webbed hands…

He came up sputtering spray and sand. The wave receded, its greedy grasp dragging him back into the sea, but he crawled forward, lurching up to stumble onto the shore, the siren song fading from his mind.

"Silas!" Abigail was there, gripping his arm, shaking him, terror honing her voice like a knife. "What in the *hell* were you doing?"

He coughed and dragged in a breath, glancing back over his shoulder at the sea. *Come to us…*

"No! Don't you dare!" Pain lanced through his shoulder as her nails latched on hard. "Don't you *dare* do that again!"

"What…" Silas turned, rubbing his sore shoulder, then his aching back. She'd attacked him, but… Then he remembered the call, the yearning, his nightmares, the tome, and Devil Reef, and he knew there was a connection. But what connection other than utter madness, he couldn't fathom. "God in heaven." His knees folded and hit the hard sand.

"What *happened* to you?" Abigail's hysteria seemed tempered now. "Were you intending to *swim* out to Devil Reef?"

"No…I just…lost myself for a second." She'd never believe him if he told her of his nightmares and the siren song pulling him in. She'd think him stark raving mad. "I remembered swimming here as a boy, and just…"

"Come on." She tugged at his arm. "You're *soaked*, and you owe me another umbrella."

"I…" Silas glanced again over his shoulder at the sea. Its call still pulled at him, but he could resist it now. He staggered with her back to the car and hurled himself into his seat. The door thumped closed, dulling the siren song of the surf. "I'm sorry. I don't know what came over me."

"Well, never mind." Abigail jammed the shifter in gear and wheeled the car around. "We've got to figure out some other way to get out to Devil Reef. Something's happening around here, and you deciding to take a *swim* in the middle of a storm corroborates my theory that it's affecting us *both*."

"Yes." He couldn't disagree but had little more to add. They couldn't get a boat in Innsmouth, and couldn't take *Sea Change* around the cape in this weather. They were done. There was nothing to do but go home.

They drove in silence, Silas's thoughts running in circles. What would have happened if Abigail hadn't broken his trance? Would he have drowned in the surf, unable to help himself? Why did he feel that the answer to the connection between his nightmares and the tome's prophecy was to be found out on Devil Reef?

"What next?" Abigail asked as Arkham hove into view.

"Next?" He barked a laugh and wiped the gritty salt from his face with the sleeve of his sodden shirt. "I have no idea, Abigail."

"Well, the end of the whole world is looming, and we know where it's going to start, Silas Marsh. We have to do *something*! We can't just run away from this!" Abigail's old determination was back, and it infected him like a fever.

No more running… "We need to think."

"Yes, we do."

"And I need a drink."

"If you mean something stronger than coffee, I'm with you."

He looked at her with surprise. "Really?"

"Yes." Abigail swallowed hard and nodded. "The end of the works of *mankind*, Silas! *Hell*, yes!"

He pointed to a diner as they neared the edge of town. "Join me, then. Maybe we'll come up with an idea."

Chapter Five

Hibb's Roadhouse

Lordy, you two are soaked right through!" the waitress said as she sauntered over. "Need a little something to warm you up?"

"Yes." Silas knew this place and knew what to order. "Two sweet iced teas with lemon."

The waitress blinked at them, but then winked and nodded. "Comin' right up, sugar."

"Sweet iced tea?" Abigail made a face. "I thought you said—"

"Trust me."

Ordering sweet iced tea with lemon wouldn't have raised an eyebrow south of the Mason-Dixon Line, but no New Englander would ever request it. Prohibition put the kibosh on the legal sale of alcohol, but that didn't mean it couldn't be gotten. Speakeasies like this one often used subtle codes to order spirited libation. In this case, "sweet iced tea with lemon" would get you Canadian whiskey on the rocks, and nobody would know the difference.

The waitress returned in moments holding two tall glasses with lemon wedges perched on the rim. "Enjoy," she said with another wink as she put the glasses on the table and sashayed off.

"Drink up." Silas lifted his glass and took a swallow. The cold Canadian whiskey burned a track of icy fire down his throat.

Abigail sniffed her glass and her eyes widened. "Sweet tea, huh." She sipped and stifled a cough. "Jesus, Mary, and Joseph, that's more like it!" She took another sip and then a deep breath. "Are you feeling any better?"

"Some." Silas stared at his drink. *She must think I'm loony, walking into the sea…* But he could still feel that call, that yearning, and the rap of the old woman's stick on the floor of the net loft reverberating through his bones.

"Those people, the Marshes…the main family…" Abigail paused as if unsure how to proceed. "Do they all have that…look?"

"Most." Silas took another big swallow and felt the whiskey start to dull his nerves, ease the pounding in his head. "It supposedly started generations back with Old Obed Marsh. Old Obed went to sea and came back with a new wife and…some strange notions. That wasn't long before a plague wiped out nearly a third of the town. Since then, the Marshes tend to keep to themselves, mostly marrying within the extended family."

"Innsmouth…" Abigail drank and hiccuped. "God above, Silas, what's happening in that town?"

"I don't know." He shook his head in honest befuddlement. "I grew up there, but I never did learn the truth. Nobody talks about it, and asking questions will only get you trouble."

"And what happened to you on that beach?"

"I…don't really know." Abigail's eyes showed only concern. She'd saved him back there, and deserved an honest answer. If she called him crazy, well, he wouldn't call her a liar. "The sea calls to me, Abigail. It always has, but lately it's been…hard to ignore. Until now, I've been able to resist. Being on my boat, on the water, helps, but there on that beach, I just…"

"*Calls* to you?" Her brow furrowed.

"I know. It sounds crazy." He drank more whiskey and sighed. "It *is* crazy."

"No crazier than a book that changes and speaks of the end of the world!" She gripped his arm hard. "What do we *do*? I'm *scared*, Silas!"

"You'd be a fool or crazy *not* to be scared. Hell, I think I *am* crazy, and I'm *still* scared."

"You're not crazy, and neither am I!" Abigail gulped from her glass and gasped a deep breath. "Look, I thought a lot on the way back. That…woman in Innsmouth didn't even flinch when I asked her what was going to happen out on Devil Reef. She *knew*!"

"Maybe, but so what?"

"Don't you see? She refused to let us borrow a boat! She stopped us from going out there!" Abigail leaned over the table. "That means we're onto something here! They're afraid we *can* do something to stop this! Just like the date in the book changing—it's changing because it *knows* we're onto it! It wouldn't be trying to stop us if we weren't a threat!"

"It?" Silas didn't like the sound of that. "Before you said 'they' knew we were onto them and were changing the date to foil us. You think my damned relatives have something to do with this, and now you're saying '*it*.' What do you mean?"

"I don't know, but something or someone's behind this, Silas. I don't know what *it* or *they* are, but something's out there on Devil Reef. It's involved with those *freaks* in Innsmouth, and it damn near dragged you into the sea this afternoon!" She gripped his arm again, her nails biting in hard. "And it intends to end the world of man!"

"But how can we stop something we don't understand?"

"I don't know that either, but if we *couldn't* stop it, would it be working so hard to try to stop *us*?" Abigail sipped her whiskey and let go of his arm. "Why fight us if we had no chance?"

That made a terrifying type of sense. Maybe they could stop it. Silas downed the rest of his whiskey and decided not to argue with her use of 'we.' He was in this now, and he knew as surely as he knew he would have swum right out to Devil Reef this afternoon if Abigail hadn't jabbed him in the back with her umbrella, that if he didn't put an end to this, he would finally succumb to that call. But if he could stop it, maybe…maybe his nightmares would end.

"Fine. We can stop this, but how?"

"We've got to get out to that reef and find out what's there, but without a boat, how can we?"

"Whoever stole my chart must have been trying to keep us from…" Every plot pricked the chart at exactly the same spot. "The location I plotted wasn't on the reef, but *behind* it! There's a slough that runs right up behind the reef! That's deep water!"

"So, now we need to look *underwater*?" Abigail's nose wrinkled in disbelief. "How in the name of—"

"Abigail, that's it! That's why whatever's behind this is worried. When I'm not fishing I work deep-sea salvage, recovering lost fishing gear or sunken boats. I've got a diving rig in Kingsport, but I can't get *Sea Change* around the cape!"

Abigail's eyes widened. "Wait! What about the canal?"

"Canal?"

"Yes, Blynman Canal, from Gloucester to Annisquam! I've seen it on maps in the library! You said you couldn't take your boat *around* Cape Ann, but the canal cuts *behind* the cape! Can't you take your boat through there?"

"Sonofa..." Silas bit off the curse. "I've never used it. The channel's narrow and shoaled, and the drawbridge is more apt to be *stuck* than working properly. I can't get *Sea Change* under it without lowering the entire mast rig, which takes hours, so I've always gone around the cape."

"But you *can* lower it, right?"

"I *suppose*, but..." Silas preferred open sea to a stinking ditch, but now, with the storm ravaging Cape Ann, it made sense. "You're right. We can do this, but we've got to hurry to get out of the Annisquam bar before the wind backs to the north. Drink up! We've got work to do!" He pushed her glass toward her. "We need to pick up that book from the library in case the date changes again, then lower the mast and get down to Kingsport before dark! You can help me run the diving rig."

"Um..." Abigail took another gulp from her glass and put it down. "Okay, but you'll have to show me what to do. I've never been on a boat in my life! I can't even *swim*!"

He blinked at her. "You can't *swim*, and you waded into the surf after me?"

Her cheeks flushed pink. "That was entirely different!"

He didn't want to argue that it really wasn't different; she'd saved his life, after all. "Well, come on." Silas dropped four bits on the table and bustled her out into the storm. "If we hurry, we can be through the Annisquam end of the canal before the tide starts to ebb."

Chapter Six

Devil Reef

Light slashed through the rain as they rounded the last bend in Blynman Canal, and Silas breathed a sigh of relief. The wind only kicked up wavelets in the narrow waterway, and the tide was still flowing in, instead of out, but that was about to change. He'd been surprised to find the tide at Blynman Bridge dead low when it should have been flooding, but that had been to their advantage. The laborious process of lowering the mast and boom had been worth it. They'd slipped under the bridge with feet to spare. The light swept like a scythe over them again, a great cyclopean eye questing through the night.

"That's Wigwam Point Light." Silas pointed. "The bar's just beyond. If the wind's backed too far to the north, it could be breaking, but we'll see. The tide seems to be flooding still, but it *should* be on the ebb! That's good for us. The storm must be causing a surge."

"I didn't understand a word you just said!" Abigail gripped the pilothouse console as if hanging on for dear life, even though the boat barely rocked. She'd changed into flat shoes, trousers, flannel shirt, and a raincoat buttoned up to her neck, hardly the prim librarian any longer. She'd asked him about life preservers, but he didn't have any. The bulky things were more likely to kill you than save you on a working fishing boat.

"That lighthouse marks the opening of the canal to the sea." Silas pointed. "If the wind's blowing from the north, the waves will be big across the mouth of the channel where it shallows. The tide's still coming in, which it *shouldn't* be doing, but that'll help. If the waves are breaking, we won't be able to pass."

"Oh." She swallowed hard. "Okay."

"Just hang on. It'll get bumpy, but *Sea Change* can take it."

She nodded and gripped harder, bracing her back against the aft bulkhead.

The run from Kingsport to Gloucester had been rough, but not dangerous. Despite her terror, Abigail had been only mildly ill. The Annisquam bar, however, would be the telling tale. The winds of a nor'easter backed from east to northeast to north as the storm progressed up the coast. If the wind had already shifted to the north, the seas would race right into the mouth of the canal, and they'd be in for a real trouncing. Passing the bar in daylight with this weather would have been dangerous enough. Silas didn't tell Abigail that doing it in the dark bordered on suicidal.

Silas squinted into the gloom as the lighthouse beam swept the sea. The swells rose across the bar in dark lines of shadow through the rain-streaked windows. They were large, but they weren't breaking. *Good timing or dumb luck, I'll take it.* He eased the throttle forward and *Sea Change* picked up speed.

The bow lifted as they mounted the first real swell, then tilted down into the trough. The next was steeper and the next even higher as they passed Wigwam Light. Silas flicked his gaze constantly between the compass and the sea. When the lighthouse beam swept past from astern, he glimpsed one of the channel buoys and altered course.

"What's that light?" Abigail's voice trembled as she pointed ahead.

"The sea buoy. It's a good reference, but the one we need to find is red number four. That one's not lit, but it marks the western shoal. Once that's behind us, we can make our turn."

Abigail bit back a squeak of terror as *Sea Change* pitched violently over a sharp swell.

"Don't worry! The waves aren't breaking!" *Thank God…* "We can make it!"

"Okay!" She didn't sound convinced.

"Just help me look for a red buoy. Doing this with only one eye isn't easy!"

"Sure!" She pressed her face closer to the rain-streaked glass.

Silas leaned out the pilothouse door and squinted into the rain as the beam of light swept the sea once more. *Nothing...* He couldn't see when they were in the trough between waves. He had to get a look when they were atop one. *Sea Change* climbed over another swell, but the light didn't sweep in time. *Come on...* Silas throttled back a bit, trying to time his progress with the light and the next wave.

A wave loomed, and the light swept the sea. Silas leaned out again and shielded his eye from the slashing rain.

"There!" Red number four shone clearly for an instant only fifty yards off their port bow.

"I see it!" Abigail sounded both panicked and triumphant.

"That buoy is our mark to turn. We're right where we need to be!" He flashed her a grin, realizing that the tension and the motion of the sea had him feeling better than he had in weeks. "We're good! We're going to make it!"

"Oh, *good*!"

They passed the buoy, and Silas watched the swells. He'd have to time his turn just right. "Hang on, now. We'll take at least one hard roll before we get pointed the right direction."

"I *am* hanging on!"

Silas counted the swells, waiting for the peak seventh in the set. They climbed over the peak swell, and he wrenched the wheel hard to port. *Sea Change* answered as they raced down the back side of the swell. The next was not so high, but it caught them on the beam, rolling the boat so far that her gunnels dipped. Something crashed across the cabin behind him—the coffee pot maybe—but he didn't have time to look. Another swell rolled them hard before her bow came around. The next they took on the quarter, lessening the roll but making steering more difficult. He fought the wheel to keep the bow down the wave and watched white water roar past.

"We're making good time now!" He grinned at Abigail, but her eyes were squeezed tightly shut. "Abigail! We're clear. We're headed for Devil Reef. Just a few miles. It's going to be roily, but in half an hour we'll be in protected waters." He steered by feel as another wave picked up their stern and they raced down a wave, keeping his eye on the compass.

"It's pitch black out! How do you know where we are?" Abigail still didn't sound convinced that they weren't in mortal danger.

"See that light?" Silas pointed to the sweeping beam far off the port bow. "That's the Innsmouth lighthouse."

"Okay."

"And that smaller light over there," he pointed to starboard, "is the Essex Bay sea buoy. We'll see the Plum Island Channel sea buoy before long and that'll mark our turn inshore. I know the compass headings through the channel by heart." He wasn't about to tell her the danger of miscalculating his approach and actually hitting one of the reefs. There was no reason to worry her any further when the careening corkscrew motion of the boat already had her terrified.

After a half hour of enduring that millrace run downwind, white water roaring down the sides of the boat at every roll, Silas pointed out the Plum Island buoy and lined up his approach. Glancing behind them at the lighted buoy, the lighthouse, and the compass, he made his turn. The seas were now on the port stern quarter, which made the steering tricky. If he took one wrong, they could broach and roll. Without a chart or his logbook, he was going from memory, but when the sweep of Innsmouth lighthouse illuminated a ghostly white line of breakers on the reefs to starboard, he knew he was in the right spot. In ten minutes, the seas calmed, and he turned north.

"We're behind the reefs." Silas eased his grip on the wheel and flexed his hands to relieve cramped muscles.

"Thank Heavens!" Abigail rubbed her eyes and blinked, peering into the darkness. "I still can't see a thing."

"I know where we are, and I know the approach to Devil Reef from inshore. It's tricky, but I've done it dozens of times." He left out the part about not having his chart.

"I thought you said the Marshes don't let anyone fish there."

"They don't." He grinned at her. "But they can't watch all the time. You can't see the reef from town unless you climb the lighthouse or drive out to the beach."

She peered out the window, then up at the sky. "What about our lights? Won't they see them?"

"Oh, hell! Thanks!" Silas flipped the switch that killed their running lights. "I forgot. I never run at night without lights."

"Nice to know I'm good for something."

"I couldn't do this without you, Abigail. This is *your* mystery, remember?"

"I wish I could forget!"

When Innsmouth light shone at the right bearing, Silas turned north and slipped between the shoals behind Devil Reef. Again, without his chart, he was going by memory. Then the light swept past to illuminate the roaring white line of the breakers on the reef.

Come to us...

So focused upon piloting through the storm, the shoals and reefs, Silas had forgotten the siren song that he felt on the beach. Now it sang along his every nerve. He gritted his teeth against that call, that yearning, and throttled back, approaching slowly. He no longer needed a chart to tell him where to go.

Almost home...yes...come to us...

"We're close." He pulled the throttle back to an idle. "I can *feel* it!"

"You can?" Abigail looked at him askance.

"Yes." They slowed until the boat came to a dead stop against the howling wind. "Steer her straight into the wind for a moment while I drop anchor."

"Okay." Abigail took the wheel tentatively.

Silas strode out onto the bow and released the anchor. It plunged down into inky blackness, running free for sixty feet before it struck bottom. He resisted the urge to dive in after it, and let out another two hundred feet before tying it off.

"We're here," he announced as he stepped back into the pilothouse and kicked the engine out of gear.

"Finally!" Abigail hurried aft to the chart table and pulled her tome from her satchel.

He joined her to peer at the page under a shuttered lantern. "Anything new?"

"Yes." She looked up at him. "The time's changed again, Silas."

"When is it now?"

"Tomorrow night, just past midnight." She jotted down a new

set of numbers in her notebook and turned to show him. "It's skipped up a whole day."

"Damn it!" An uncharacteristic surge of anger welled up as if he'd just seen the second ace of hearts in a deck of cards. "Ever feel like we're being flimflammed?"

"What, like this is just an elaborate trick or something?" Abigail blinked and shook her head. "No. You saw the numbers in the book change. That's no trick."

"I know, but what if..." His anger evolved into a cold dread in his gut. "Twelve hours ago, I walked into the surf because this place was calling to me. Now here I am, ready to get in the water. Maybe that's exactly what it *wants* me to do."

"What it *wants* you to do?" Confusion furrowed her brow.

"Yes! I can *still* feel it calling me, Abigail!" Silas clenched his scarred hands into fists. "Maybe we're not *preventing* anything. Maybe that book's lying to us, or whatever *is* going to bring about this end of the world needs *me* to do it! Maybe *it* sent you to me!"

"Silas, I... You don't think that I'm trying to—"

"No! No, Abigail, not you. You saved me on that beach, but that book," he stabbed a finger at the tome, "could just be a...a tool or a piece of something bigger that wants me to go down there."

"But if you don't go, and we *can* prevent this..."

"Or that's what it wants and I help bring an end to the world!"

She shook her head. "I don't believe it. A four hundred-year-old prophecy just to lure *you* into the water?"

"Unless it needs me to fulfill that prophecy!" Silas gritted his teeth against the call of the sea that sang through his bones. "Damned if I do, and damned if I don't." He closed his eyes and saw the grinning teeth of the old woman in Innsmouth. "I feel like if I go down there, I'll never come back."

"Silas, *I* was the one who discovered this passage, not you." Abigail thumped a finger to the text, and Silas would have sworn the figures in the margin writhed. "I asked you to help me, but I also asked about a dozen others. Everyone else thought I was crazy, and *you* believed me. That's not a trick. That's being human: a real, honest-to-God human being willing to lay down his life for someone he only met two days ago! That's why you're here—not because of some curse."

He opened his mouth but didn't have anything to say. Her trust in him, her faith in his humanity, cut through his fear like a knife.

"Besides," she continued, "if that *revolting* old woman in Innsmouth tried to stop us from coming out here, we *have* to be on the right track!"

Silas swallowed and nodded. She had a point. "All right." He flexed his big hands, looked down at his scarred palms, and took a breath. "All right, then, come on. I need to get the mast and boom back in place, and show you how to work the compressor and lift."

Opening the engine compartment, he threw the lever that diverted power from the gearbox to the winch. An hour of dangerous labor later, the mast and boom were once again up, their cables cinched down tight. Finally, he stepped out on deck to show Abigail how to work the controls.

"It's just like a car. Pull the clutch and shift up or down to spool the line in or out. If there's tension on the line, and you pull the clutch, it'll spool out, just like a car coasting downhill."

"Okay."

"The compressor's simple." He jerked the pull start and it sputtered to life. "Keep gas in the tank there and it'll run forever. Just don't kink the air hose."

"Right."

"There's also a telephone setup so we can talk." He pointed to the simple box propped against the side of the cabin out of the rain. "You can tell me if anything goes wrong, and I can tell you what I'm seeing."

"Well, *that's* a help." She experimented with the phone as he shrugged into the heavy breastplate and massive boots.

Silas clomped back inside the cabin and opened the locker, grabbed his heavy knife and clipped it to the belt of his dive suit. The light from Innsmouth lighthouse swept over the boat to glint on cold blue metal in the back of the locker.

Better safe than sorry. Silas pulled the Remington from its bracket and a box of shells from the shelf. "You know how to use this?"

Abigail looked at the shotgun dubiously. "In theory, but why would I need a firearm?"

Silas nodded to the lighthouse as he broke open the breech and checked the loads. "Someone might see us from the lighthouse. If they do, and Old Man Marsh hears that there's someone out here, they might send a boat out to run us off." He propped the Remington in the corner just inside the cabin door. "If you have to use it, just remember to hold it tight against your shoulder and don't aim below our waterline. Double-aught buckshot'll put a hole right through her hull, and then we'll be in a real pickle. Now, help me with the helmet."

Abigail bit her lip and nodded. "Sure."

They muscled the heavy helmet over his head and sealed it to the suit, but Silas left the faceplate open for now. He picked up the powerful dive lantern and briefly flipped the switch to check the battery while Abigail hooked the lift line to the eye bolt on the top of the helmet. He shuffled to the rail and sat down. With weights, boots, and helmet, the rig weighed about two hundred pounds, so he couldn't go anywhere fast. Once in the water, he'd be able to move easier.

"Check the telephone."

"Right." Abigail cranked the handle and spoke into the microphone. "Can you hear me?"

Her voice crackled in his ear. "Yes, I hear you fine." His own crackly voice came out of the telephone speaker. "Okay, we're in about sixty feet of water, and there's two hundred feet of hose coiled on deck. I'll have to search around, so if I come near the end, just let me know."

"Right." She pointed to his nose and smiled weakly. "Don't forget the faceplate."

"I'd be in for a shock if I did." He closed the plate and dogged it down tight. The outside world vanished from his senses. No howling wind, slashing rain, lapping water, only the echo of his fear and the siren call pulling him into the depths. *Just do it, Silas.* He adjusted the air flow, and said, "Okay, I'm ready. Lift me up. I can't climb over the rail in this rig."

"Okay." She worked the lever that engaged the lift, and he felt the weight leave his shoulders. The straps of the suit pulled him up, and he braced a foot against the rail to keep from swinging.

The familiar tasks of getting everything ready had settled his nerves, but now that it came to actually descending into that inky blackness, terror rose up like bile from his gut.

"Be careful," Abigail's voice crackled.

"Careful?" Silas barked a nervous laugh, marshaled his flagging courage, and pushed off the railing. With nothing beneath him but water, he said, "Down."

"Down," came her reply.

Silas descended into blackness.

He flipped on the light, but the beam vanished into the hazy distance no matter which way he directed it. He turned his head inside the helmet, but with only one eye he couldn't see out the back left porthole. There was also no way to look straight down with the tension of the line keeping him upright. Cold crept up his legs as the suit pressed in on him like a chill embrace. He adjusted the air flow, yawning to pop his ears, and the chill receded.

"Forty…fifty…sixty…" Abigail's crackly voice called off the marks on the winch line, his only link to the world of air and light.

His boots hit something, and he staggered as the weight of the helmet came down on his shoulders, less than it was on the surface, but still heavy. "Stop. I'm on the bottom." He shone the light around. Silt billowed up around his legs in an obscuring cloud. A few sleepy fish and one lobster skittered among the algae-covered rocks. Nothing unusual. "I can see only about twenty feet. The water's all churned up from the storm. I'm going to start walking a big circle, so give me some slack."

"How much?" He could barely hear her over the roar of the surf on the reef and his pounding heart.

"Twenty feet at a time." Silas began trudging forward. "I'll walk out until it comes taut then do a circle." His shuffling steps stirred up even more silt, obscuring his view. "If I don't find anything, you give me twenty more and I do it again."

"Right."

Silas shuffled along until the lift line pulled him up short. He shone the light around, twisting back and forth in the cumbersome suit for a better view. With only one eye, he had to turn his whole body to look to his left. The inky blackness yielded nothing but indistinct shapes that flicked at the limit of his vision. *Just fish attracted to the light.* He swallowed the lump in his throat, turned to his left, and continued along, all but blind.

Come to us…

"What?" Silas stopped and rapped his helmet. "What did you say?"

"I didn't say anything," came Abigail's reply.

"I thought—" He jerked to a stop as his light reflected off something silvery, snapped his head around inside the helmet to look, but it was gone. His heart hammered in his ears, his mouth suddenly dry. Silas swung the light around frantically. Nothing. "Talk to me, Abigail. I…need to hear a voice."

"Oh, okay. You're between the boat and the reef. You didn't walk in a circle. You walked straight toward the reef."

"I did?" He turned left to walk a circle.

No…come to us…come home.

He stopped. The voice wasn't Abigail, and turning his back on it felt like pressing a knife into his own flesh. His legs refused to take a step. He turned back and shone the light, but still there was nothing there.

"Give me some more slack, Abigail. I can…feel it. It's calling me."

"Silas? You sound strange!"

He shook his head sharply. Sweat dripped off his nose. "I'm okay." He wasn't okay, not by a long shot. "Talk to me. Hearing your voice helps. Just give me slack."

"Okay."

The line slackened and Silas trudged forward, sweeping the light back and forth. *Nothing…*

Abigail's voice crackled, "Ninety feet…one hundred…"

When she reached one hundred fifty, a dark wall of riveted iron loomed out of the blackness.

Silas stopped. "I found something!" He shone his light up the wall to illuminate a porthole and a railing high above, bending his back to look up through the helmet's portholes. "A shipwreck. A freighter, maybe." He started toward it, but the line jerked him to a stop. "Slack."

"Okay, slack." The tension eased. "Be careful, Silas!"

Careful…right. Silas gritted his teeth to keep them from chattering and shuffled forward. The light illuminated a jagged hole in the side of the ship, the thick iron bent inward. Something glittered within, a flick of motion, silvery, then nothing. "There's a hole in the hull. She must have struck a mine during the war."

The air hose yanked him back hard, nearly toppling him backward. "Slack on the hose! Is the boat drifting?"

"I *am* giving slack, and no, I don't think we've moved at all.

You're taking more air hose than rope. I don't..." Her voice crackled and started to break up.

"Abigail?" It didn't make sense that he was taking more hose than rope unless the hose had gotten hooked on a rock or something. He grabbed the hose and pulled, struggling toward the ship.

Yes...come home...

Abigail's voice crackled. "...don't know...something...with the..."

"Bad connection! You're breaking up! Crank the phone again!" The hose went slack, and he nearly fell with the release. He lunged forward in the cumbersome suit, the dark hole yawning in his light like a toothed maw. Another flicker of silver within.

"Something's pulling...end of the...to do!"

"What?" Silas tugged on the hose, lurching forward.

Yes...come...come home...

"Just a bit more!" Two more steps and he reached the gaping hole.

Grasping the edge, Silas leaned in and raised his lamp to shine inside. The light scattered a school of small fish. Larger shapes filled the space beyond, a mass of pale bodies vague through the hazy water. They rolled and roiled in a confusing swarm.

Come... Come to us... Come home.

A shape darted forth into the light, and Silas's breath caught in his throat. Bulging eyes and pointed translucent teeth, human hands with webbed fingers and claws. He panned the light, illuminating hundreds of the grotesque faces, all staring at him.

Come to us!

The call reverberated through his skull, drowning his panic, grasping his very soul, pulling him in, impossible to resist.

Carefully grasping the edge of jagged metal, Silas hauled himself up onto the edge. A piercing, crackling scream sang in his ears, but he ignored it. He scrabbled over the edge into the wreck, finally answering the siren call.

Come home... Home.

Something jerked Silas backward so hard he cracked his forehead on the helmet. As he fell backward through the jagged hole, the beam of his light swept up into the rusty iron frames of the wreck's hold. Something larger loomed there, something inconceivable, huge and writhing, eyes as big as platters, tentacles with clawed tips. At the center of the nightmare, a maelstrom of darkness within darkness swallowed his light like a hungry maw.

Then he was lying on his back, a full ten feet from the opening. Before he could even try to get up, he was dragged back over the rough rocks then jerked upright toward the surface. A scream crackled from the telephone. *Abigail?* She was hauling in the lift line. Something must have happened.

Silas surged from the water and into the air, his helmet clanging against the boom pulley as he jerked to a stop. A deafening boom split the air with a flash like lightning.

Dangling like a side of beef in a butcher shop, unable to get down, Silas played his light over the deck. Abigail sat against the cabin bulkhead, the smoking Remington in her lap. Some feet away, a shape lay sprawled on the deck. Abigail stared wide-eyed at the thing, trembling, her finger still tight on the triggers of the shotgun.

"Abigail!" he yelled, but either the phone line was out, or she couldn't hear it. He considered cutting the lift line, but with the boom out over the water, that would send him plunging back down into the depths. Instead, he worked the dogs of his faceplate and swung the tiny window open. "Abigail!"

She jerked and looked up at him as if stunned that he'd somehow levitated into the air. Realization dawned on her face, and she scrambled up. Her hands shook as she put aside the smoking shotgun and worked the crank to swing the lift boom inboard. As she eased the clutch and lowered Silas gently to the deck, he noticed that the engine wasn't running. The sudden stop of the lift must have killed it.

"Silas!" Abigail helped him with the helmet, her face pale and dripping in the rain. "Silas what *is* that! It climbed up your air hose! It tried to…to *grab* me!"

Finally, the helmet came off and he could see. One of the creatures he'd seen inside the wreck lay splayed on the deck, a smoking hole as big as Silas's fist in its chest. Once free of the cumbersome suit, he crossed the deck and knelt by the dead creature.

"I don't know what it is, Abigail, but…"

Half-fish, half-human, it reminded him of the illustrations in Abigail's tome. *My nightmares…* Its thick lips, wide mouth, bulging eyes, and sloped forehead bore an unsettling resemblance to the old woman in Innsmouth. *The main Marsh family...* Silas poked the cold, scaly flesh with a finger and shuddered. He couldn't deny what he'd seen in the wreck now, not with the proof lying before him. He wasn't crazy. *The family curse isn't madness, it's* this!

"It tried to *grab* me, Silas!" Abigail whirled and snatched up the Remington, snapping open the breech and loading two more shells from her pocket. "It climbed up your air hose!"

"There are *more* of them down there, Abigail." Silas gritted his teeth against the call echoing in his mind, the memory of those writhing shapes. He strode into the cabin, pulled the bottle of spiritus frumenti from the cupboard, and wrenched the cork free. The whiskey burned a line down his throat. "Here." He traded the bottle for the shotgun.

Abigail drank down two swallows, coughed, and said, "*More* of them?" The bottle quaked in her hand as she handed it back. "How many more?"

"I didn't *count* them! A *lot* more." *Enough to drag us down there.* He handed her the Remington and took the bottle back, the memory of what else he'd seen screaming through his mind. *Got to get the hell out of here.* Replacing the bottle in the cupboard, he went back on deck and started hauling in the air hose. "And something else. Something bigger and...darker. I don't know. I only got a glimpse."

"Bigger?" Abigail stood in the doorway out of the rain, the shotgun steadier now in her grasp.

"Yes, a *lot* bigger! And some kind of...maelstrom, or something." When he had the air hose hauled in, Silas killed the compressor and glared down at the slimy corpse on the deck. Loath to touch it, he pulled on a pair of thick gloves and heaved the disgusting thing over the side. The rain would wash the vile creature's blood and slime away by the time they got back. He threw his gloves overboard and stepped past Abigail into the cabin. "Keep an eye out while I get the engine started and haul anchor. We'll be out of here in ten minutes!"

"What? Where are we going?"

"Home, Arkham, anywhere! As far the *hell* away from here as possible!" Silas heaved open the engine room hatch, flipped the transfer coupling back to the drive shaft, and cranked the engine to life.

"Wait!"

"For what, one of those monsters to come up here and drag us down to Davey Jones's Locker?" He slammed the hatch and started forward.

"Listen to me!" She followed him to the pilothouse, still holding the shotgun. "Nothing's *changed*, Silas! We still have to stop this!"

"Stop it?" He whirled on her. "There's no *way*, Abigail! Those things are huge! We've got to get away!"

"Away where? Don't you remember the passage? All the works of man will be cast down! Everything! You *can't* run away from that!" She wasn't exactly pointing the Remington at him, but at the deck between them. Her finger rested very near the triggers.

This is crazy! She's crazy! Silas's nightmares had become real. There were monsters beneath them right now, a seething mass of horrors that called to him even as they argued, and she wanted him to dive down there and take them all on with nothing but a belt knife! Terror pounded through his veins, drowning out the siren call. If he moved quickly, he might get the gun from her before she blasted a hole through the deck and maybe even the hull, but what then?

The end of the world of man… Armageddon. No place to hide.

"*How*, Abigail? How do we stop this? I *can't* go down there again!"

"What? Why not?"

"*Because*, damn it! You remember the beach! Remember me walking into the damnable ocean? They called to me when I was down there, Abigail, and I couldn't resist. If you hadn't pulled me up, I'd have walked right into the whole swarming mass of them!"

She stumbled back half a step, her face as white as a sheet. "Then the world's doomed, Silas. I can't do this without your help, and you won't help. You're dooming millions by doing nothing."

"There's nothing *to* do!"

"Isn't there?" She stepped forward. "You're telling me there's no way to blow that wreck to hell? Gasoline? Dynamite? Anything?"

"We don't *have* anything like that!" He needed to make her see reason. She hadn't seen what he'd seen. "And even if we did, we don't know if it'll work! If I go back down there, I'll *die*!"

"We *do* know! We *must* be able to stop this or they wouldn't be trying so hard to stop us! If we don't destroy that evil place, we *both* die! All of *mankind* dies! Don't you see?"

Silas gritted his teeth. *The end of the world of man...* He whirled away from her and leaned on the boat's wheel, gazing out into the howling darkness, trying to think through his terror.

Light swept over them from the Innsmouth lighthouse, drawing his eye out of habit. *Innsmouth...* Could they get something there, barrels of gasoline, maybe, and some way to get them down to the wreck and set them off? No, gasoline would float. Barrels of it would be too hard to weigh down. *We'd need a bomb, a case of TNT, or...* Memories of Innsmouth and the ships they'd seen in the harbor popped into his head, the derelict relics of the war waiting to be scrapped, and the gaping hole in the wreck beneath them.

"Sonofa—!"

"What?"

Silas turned to face Abigail. "I know where we can get something that should do the job."

"Where? What do you mean?"

"Innsmouth!" He pointed to the gleaming lighthouse. "We've got to go back to Innsmouth."

Abigail looked out the window at the lighthouse and swallowed hard. "All right. Tell me what to do."

"I can't navigate the channel until dawn, but I'd just as soon haul anchor now before more of those things climb aboard." He pointed to the Remington in her hands. "Put that away, but don't unload it. My relatives are *not* going to be happy to see us."

Chapter Seven

Innsmouth Harbor

Silas guided *Sea Change* deftly through the treacherous channel into Innsmouth Harbor with the first torpid light of dawn. The nor'easter still howled, but the wind had backed to the north in the last few hours. The storm was passing.

Innsmouth had not miraculously transformed since yesterday. The dismal, dilapidated buildings glared at them as if murderous intent lurked in their windows. It might, for all Silas knew.

"You're sure about this?" Abigail asked, biting her lip.

"No, but we should be in and out of here before anyone even knows we've arrived." Silas throttled back and turned *Sea Change* toward a derelict minelayer left over from the war. Eighty feet of rust-streaked iron, she lay with her keel buried in silt, her hull slowly rotting away. "That's the one we want. I remember hearing that she had her last load aboard when she grounded here. The war was nearly over, and the Navy was too busy to care about one old converted fishing trawler. The Marsh family claimed her as salvage, of course."

"And you think the mines are still aboard?"

"Probably. Thousands of mines were deployed in New England waters during the war. The government defused and buried the ones they never deployed. They're not worth much, dangerous to scrap, since they're packed with TNT, and the Marsh family didn't need the money. They salvaged what they wanted from the ship, and left it to rust."

"But will they still work after so long?" Abigail sounded dubious.

"As long as water didn't get inside them, they should."

"But if they see us out here fiddling with it..." Abigail cast a nervous look toward shore.

"They'll try to stop us." Silas pulled alongside and brought them to a stop. "That's what the shotgun's for."

He stepped out of the cabin and tied them to the derelict so he could cast off quickly if they had visitors.

"We'll need the lift." Silas opened the engine room and worked the power transfer lever, but left the hatch open. "As soon as we get the mine aboard, I'll shift her back, and we'll get out of here."

"Good." Abigail propped the Remington just inside the cabin door. "I'd rather we didn't have to kill anyone."

"Me too, but if they pick a fight, I'll not back down." After facing the horrors of Devil Reef, a confrontation with his monstrous relatives seemed less daunting. This was something he *could* fight, unlike what he'd seen in that sunken ship. Silas cranked the winch until the boom hung over the deck of the rusty ship. "Give a yell if you see anyone coming and be ready on the winch."

Silas grabbed a crowbar and the weighted clip on the end of the lift rope, and clambered aboard the derelict ship. She'd been a steam-powered fishing trawler before the war, taken by the military to lay mines around New England. The hatch to the main hold looked intact, which was both good and bad. The ship's cargo had been kept out of the weather, but he'd have to break in.

The lock on the hatch was as big as his palm and caked with rust, but no match for a crowbar and the expertly applied force of a desperate sailor. The pieces clanked to the deck, and Silas hooked the lift rope to the hatch cover.

"Up on the lift, Abigail. I've got to get the hatch cover off."

"Right." She engaged the winch, and the heavy rope came taut.

Rusty iron hinges screeched, but the hatch cover lifted free. When it was almost vertical, he yelled "Stop", then pushed it past the tipping point and waved for her to lower it. He unclipped the line and took it to the hatch.

The muted predawn light barely illuminated the depths of the hold, but as his vision adjusted, he discerned six black, bulbous shapes resting in a wooden frame. *Like eggs in a basket.*

"Slack the lift!" Silas called, and lowered the hook into the hold until it neared the bottom. "Stop!" Silas climbed up onto the hatch coaming, wrapped a leg around the lift line, and stepped off into the open hatch. The heavy rope bit into his calloused palms as he lowered himself into the hold's dark confines.

Eerily quiet after the howling winds above, the hold felt close and smelled of mold. *Not good…* Mold meant moisture, which meant corrosion. In fact, rust streaked the edge of the hatch, and water had dripped right down onto two of the mines. A quick inspection told him they were ruined, the threaded holes that had held the fuses were full of water and rust. The next two were dry, but when Silas swiped a finger down into one of the fuse holes, it came back with flakes of grime and rust.

"Damn!"

The last two he could barely see in the dim light. His finger probed the fuse holes and came back dry and reasonably clean. The trouble now was that the other mines were in the way. If he hooked the lift to the one he wanted, it would bowl the others out of their cradles when he lifted it. The mines *shouldn't* explode without fuses, but hundreds of pounds of iron-bound explosives rolling around the inside of a ship's hold wasn't healthy. The only option was to lift the other mines out of the way first.

"Nothing for it." Silas hooked the lift cable to the first mine and climbed up hand over hand, swinging easily over the hatch coaming. "Abigail! I've got to move some cargo out of the way. Listen for my instructions!" *Best not to tell her what kind of cargo…*

"Hurry! I see some people on one of the docks looking at us!"

Silas squinted to the north. Several figures clustered on the Marsh Fish Products pier. *Not good…* "Okay, up on the lift!"

Abigail threw the lever and the rope came taut. The motor lugged with the effort, but the first mine lifted out of the cradle and swung free. Silas pushed the rope to keep it from slamming into the bulkhead, but it was like trying to hold back a falling tree. Iron boomed with the impact, and he cringed. *Well, if it explodes, I won't have to go back down to that cursed wreck anyway.*

"Down!"

Abigail complied, and iron boomed again as the mine dropped against the hull.

"Hold there!" Silas climbed down, switched the cable to the next mine in the way, and climbed back up. "Okay, up!"

The lift line came tight against the hatch coaming, the stout rope riding over the sharp lower edge and peeling away flakes of rust. The mine came free of the cradle and swung, hitting the forward bulkhead hard enough to dent it.

"What are you *doing*?" Abigail called.

"Moving cargo, just like I said!" He glanced back at the fishing pier. Six figures were climbing down onto a boat. Silas yelled, "No time to be gentle! Down!"

The mine boomed to the deck below, and Silas slid down the line. He unclipped the hook and pulled it aft. "Slack!" Clicking the hook onto the lift ring, he looked up to where the rope would ride over the edge of the hatch coaming. Rusty iron offered a dangerously sharp edge. If it broke the lift line, they were sunk.

Need something… Silas cast about the hold, looking for an old jacket or piece of canvas, anything he could put between the line and the coaming to keep it from chafing.

"Silas! They're coming!"

No time for this! Silas tore off his shirt and wedged it between the lift line and the sharp corner of the hatch coaming. "Up!"

The line snapped taut, straining to pull the mine out of the wooden cradle. Four hundred pounds of iron and TNT cracked free and swung forward. Silas scrambled out of the way and cringed as the thing crashed against the forward bulkhead. At the noise, Abigail stopped lifting.

Silas scrambled up the rope, leapt to the deck, and waved to her. "Up!" Beyond *Sea Change*, a boat left the Marsh pier.

Abigail flipped the lever, and the mine rose. Silas guided it out of the hatch and then leapt down to *Sea Change*'s deck. "Hold on there. We've got to move the boom over, but we can't let it swing. I'll work the boom crank. As soon as it's clear of the rail, lower it to the deck."

"Okay." Abigail glanced over her shoulder, her face white. "Are you sure it won't explode?"

"No, but it hasn't yet, and we bashed it around pretty hard."

Silas worked the crank and watched the deadly weight swing out over *Sea Change*. If something broke, the mine would plunge right through the deck and maybe even the hull. Abigail slipped the clutch, and the mass of iron came down hard, but not catastrophically, to rest against the port side rail. Silas unclipped the lift line, secured it, and cast off.

"Get on the wheel, Abigail." Silas lunged for the engine room and slammed the power transfer over to power the propeller shaft.

"The *wheel*? I can't—"

"Just steer out the way we came in!" Silas slammed the engine room hatch closed and flung the gear shift into forward. "I've got to deal with my blasted *relatives*!" He grabbed the Remington, pocketed a handful of shells, and stepped out onto the deck as *Sea Change* screeched alongside the old hulk into open water. Abigail turned before they'd cleared the wreck, and the port aft rail slewed around to splinter against the ship's hull.

"Sorry! I told you I couldn't steer a boat!" came Abigail's cry.

"Don't worry about it! Just drive it like a car! The red lever's the gas pedal!"

"Oh! Well, I can do *that*!" The engine revved up, and she roared for the channel under full power.

Silas cringed at the engine's high-pitched howl. "Don't fail me now, girl!"

As they came on course for the channel, the approaching boat charged after them. Six people crowded the aft deck, and at least one stood in the wheelhouse. Several had the unmistakable wide mouth and bulging eyes of the main Marsh family.

As the pursuit narrowed, a broad-shouldered man stepped onto the foredeck of the boat, pointed to the minelayer, and shouted. "That's private property, you thieving bastard!"

"It belongs to the Marsh family, and I'm a Marsh!" Silas raised the shotgun to show them he meant business. "I'm not taking anything that's worth anything to you, so bear off!"

"You're a thief! Now heave to or we'll board you and take back what's ours!" The boat closed at a steep angle.

"You try, and you'll have a talk with Mister Remington!" Silas aimed the shotgun just off their bow and fired one barrel.

The man on the bow cursed and ducked into the pilothouse. Silas reloaded the spent round, but his warning shot proved no deterrent, for the boat full of his relatives bore on.

Silas leveled the Remington at the pilothouse. "Bear off or I swear I'll blow you to hell!"

The boat continued on a collision course.

Put up or shut up, Silas. "I warned you!" He aimed at the pilothouse windows and pulled both triggers.

Buckshot ripped through wood and shattered glass, but the pilot had ducked behind the console and popped up unharmed. On they came.

Silas fumbled to reload but knew he wouldn't get another round off before they hit. "Hang on, Abigail! Steer to port!"

"Port? What port?"

"Left!" Silas grabbed a guy-wire as the two boats collided.

The deck lurched with the impact, and Abigail screeched a word he'd never thought a librarian would utter. They veered hard to port, and Silas heard a deep rumble from behind. He whirled in time to see the mine rolling across the canted deck at him. His reflex was to leap out of the way, but a deeper dread gripped his heart at the thought of so much weight crashing into the bulwarks. If the mine broke through, it would plunge to the bottom of the harbor. Their entire plan would go straight to hell, and the world of man with it.

Silas dropped the Remington and braced his feet against the bulwark, flinging out both hands to slow the massive sphere of iron. *Idiot!* he thought just before the mine slammed him backward, pinning him against the bulwark. Something cracked, and pain lanced up his leg, a hoarse scream escaping his clenched teeth. Then *Sea Change* leveled out, and the weight of the mine eased enough for him to roll it off his leg. That hurt even more than the initial impact, and he crumpled to the deck.

"Silas! They're coming back!"

"Steer for the red buoy!" he bellowed, sitting up to peer over the splintered gunnel.

His relatives were charging at them on a collision course again, but not at such a steep angle as before. They held billy clubs and net hooks. They were going to board *Sea Change*, and from their expressions, they weren't interested in negotiating.

Scrabbling for the shotgun, he slammed two shells into the breech and cracked it closed. At the rate they were closing, he would only get one shot. Silas leveled the Remington over the gunnel and took aim. At such a short range he could easily kill two of them, but that would only ensure his fate. The others would swarm aboard, and with a broken leg, Silas couldn't stop them.

Or can I?

Silas lowered his aim and fired both barrels at the waterline of the approaching boat, blasting a hole in the hull bigger than his two clenched fists. Seawater rushed into the small boat, and she lurched, but momentum brought her crashing into *Sea Change*.

Silas staggered up onto his one good leg and flipped the Remington around, gripping the twin barrels like a club. The Marsh boat heeled with the inrushing water and the men on her deck staggered, uncertainty clear in their eyes. The big man who had shouted from the bow brandished a net hook and lunged across the gap, but Silas swung the Remington like Babe Ruth aiming for the center field wall and connected with his assailant's thick jaw. The man spun like a top, blood and teeth spraying, and started to fall between the boats. Three of his companions grabbed for him, one even sinking a net hook into his arm to keep him from falling. The others fell back, less enthused now about leaping aboard *Sea Change*.

Suddenly a horrendous screech tore from the belly of the Marshes' boat, and steam billowed briefly from the exhaust stack. The engine died, and the boat fell immediately behind, listing badly. The incoming water had evidently reached the engine's air intake.

Silas took a step before remembering his injury. His leg felt like someone was twisting a knife in it, but it supported his weight. *Maybe it's not so bad…*

Using the Remington as a crutch, he hobbled into the cabin and yelled, "Throttle back a bit. We're clear."

"Thank the Lord!" Abigail glanced back at him, her knuckles white on the wheel. "I don't know where I'm going!"

Silas limped up beside her and peered out the pilothouse window through the rain. They were close to the channel, but not close enough. "Steer right about ten degrees. See the compass there. We put that red buoy on our left but pass it close. There's a shoal to the right that's not marked. Then…" He hissed in a breath as a wave rocked the boat and his leg twisted. He grabbed the edge of the console to keep from falling.

"What happened?" Abigail altered course as he'd directed, glancing down at his leg.

"That damn heavy mine rolled and pinned my leg to the bulwark. I think something's broken." He pointed to the next mark. "That green can. Put it to our right, then turn northeast by the compass. We'll get the anchor down and I'll have a look at my leg."

"But…" Abigail bit her lip and nodded. "Right. First things first…"

"Exactly." Silas pointed to the northeast as they rounded the green can. "We'll anchor well away from the reef until we're ready. I don't want to be close to those things until we have to be."

"I can't argue with that!"

"Then we have to talk," Silas continued. "I can't walk. We'll have to figure out some way for you to manage the dive suit."

"What?" She gaped at him. "You can't be serious! I know nothing about it! The suit's too heavy! It won't fit me!"

"Then we're in trouble." Silas's head spun and his leg throbbed in time with his heart. "Just about a quarter mile more, and we'll… put the…anchor down."

"Are you okay?"

"No! That's what I've been telling you!" Silas peered down at his leg and cringed. His pants were tight from the knee down. "If I don't get my leg up soon, I'm afraid…I'm going to…pass out."

Chapter Eight

Devil Reef

They anchored in shallow water behind a shoal east of Devil Reef with little difficulty. This put them far enough from Innsmouth that the sheets of slashing rain hid them from view, but near enough to the reef that they could still see the line of breakers. Unless someone climbed the lighthouse or drove out to the beach, the Marshes should think they were long gone. Silas sat down with his leg on the chart table, and Abigail split his pant leg with a pair of shears. She hissed an indrawn breath. From knee to ankle his leg was hugely swollen.

"Well, the fibula is certainly broken, but you were able to stand on it, so I think the tibia is intact."

"What?" Silas took a pull from the bottle of spiritus frumenti and grimaced as she pulled off his boot.

"Basic anatomy." She smiled thinly. "I read a lot. Part of being a librarian, I guess."

"Oh."

"You've two bones in your leg here, and the smaller one's broken. Fortunately, the larger is the one that supports most of the weight. If we splint it so it doesn't twist, you should be able to walk." She looked around. "I need some slats of wood and cloth to bind it up."

"The locker there's got a couple of swabs…er…mops. You can

use the handles. And there's bed sheets in the fo'c'sle." He took another pull from the bottle.

"Okay, but not too much more of that." Abigail pointed at the bottle of whiskey. "You need your wits about you."

"Wits..." He shook his head. "I've already *lost* my wits just considering this madness."

Abigail ignored him and bustled about, tearing a sheet into strips and breaking two swab handles into shorter lengths for splints. As she wrapped his leg tight, Silas bit back all the curses he'd learned in two decades at sea and marveled at her.

"How do you know how to split a leg?"

"I read a lot, remember?" She cinched a knot and started wrapping another strip.

"Good. Maybe you can figure out a way to set that mine off, then." He pointed the neck of the whiskey bottle to the massive sphere of iron on the deck.

"What do you mean?" Abigail continued to work but looked at him worriedly. "I thought we just dropped it over the side and... boom."

So, librarians don't know everything after all. "No. Mines have fuses." He winced as she drew the wrappings tight. "Prongs that stick out so when a ship hits them, it sets off the mine."

"How do they work, these fuses?"

"No idea, but they're soft, made of lead. I worked on a cargo steamer during the war that transported hundreds of mines to England. They showed us they were safe as long as they didn't have fuses. The inside of the hole they screw into looks like the inside of a flashlight, two metal terminals, so I think when the fuse is bent it makes an electrical connection that sets off a charge inside."

"That can't be." She pointed out to the rain-soaked deck. "Water conducts electricity. If that's all it took, the mine would have already exploded."

"Huh...that's right."

"So maybe it needs a current to set it off, like a demolitionist's blasting cap."

Maybe..." Silas considered. "Maybe once the mine's placed I could use my lantern battery and some wire to set it off." Of course, he'd have to be right next to the mine when he did that. *Death by explosion, Armageddon, or answer the siren call of those things…not much of a choice, Silas.*

"Placed? What do you mean?"

"The mine needs to be placed *inside* the wreck."

"Why?"

"A blast outside might not do the job. The ship's hull is thick iron. Also, *unlike* the wreck, *Sea Change* is wood. If that mine blows up under her, it'll rupture the hull."

"Oh." Abigail bit her lip and cinched the final knot. "Well, then we'll just have to figure out a way to set it off from up here after you come back up, won't we?"

"That won't work. Even if we had enough wire to reach the boat, there's not enough current in that light to overcome that much resistance. I'll have to trigger it from down there."

"And blow yourself up?" She grimaced and reached for his boot. "There's *got* to be a better way, Silas."

"What *else* will work?" He was sick of arguing with her.

His boot wouldn't fit over his swollen foot, but when he stood and put careful pressure on his leg, it held his weight, although it hurt like blazes.

"Wait…" Abigail looked around. "How does the telephone work when you're down that far, then?"

"The phone box has magnetos that generate alternating current."

She looked at him blankly.

"You read a lot and you don't know about *electricity*?"

Her face reddened. "I read about ancient history, natural history, and advances in medicine, Silas. Nobody can read *everything*!"

"Sorry. The batteries in my light provide direct current, which weakens over a long wire run. Alternating current, like the lights in your house, overcomes resistance better—" He stopped cold and stared at Abigail wide-eyed. "That's *it*! The telephone! We can rig wire from the telephone box! Abigail, you're a genius!"

"I thought you said we didn't have enough wire to reach."

"We don't, and we'll need the telephone. Damn!"

"Why do we need the telephone?"

"So I can tell you how to maneuver the boat. There's no way we can anchor in exactly the right spot, so you'll have to steer *Sea Change* at anchor when I'm down there. But maybe…" Silas looked around the cabin. He had some spare wire—not enough—but there *was* more wire aboard. "We can scavenge it! If we rip out the running lights and cabin lights, we should have enough!"

"But we have no way to make sure it'll work." Abigail looked at the black iron sphere resting against the splintered rail. "Do we?"

"Not short of blowing ourselves up, no." He shrugged helplessly. "But at least we've got a chance now." *A chance to survive, and maybe to be free of this damn thing in my head...* For even now the siren call of Devil Reef cried out to him.

But would he be able to resist that call when he descended into the wreck? *If I can't, Abigail will detonate the mine, and that'll be the end of it.*

"Come on. We've got a lot of work to do, and I can't crawl around in the bilges scavenging wire."

Recovering enough wire took hours. They ate the last of a stale loaf of bread slathered with salted butter and pots of double-strength coffee to keep going. Neither had slept in more than a day, and fatigue dragged at them. Abigail was covered in filth and dead on her feet when they finally had enough wire, but the work still wasn't done. They spliced the ends of the short lengths together, dipping the splices in hot decking tar and wrapping them with tape. Silas checked the connections by hooking the wire to the telephone and touching the wires together while Abigail cranked the box. A bright blue spark arced between the wires. Connecting the wires to the mine and filling the fuse orifice with tar swallowed more precious time. Silas worked with his injured leg up as much as possible, but the pain wore on him like a beast gnawing at his gut.

All the while, they both cast glances at the rain-shrouded tower of Innsmouth lighthouse. The Marshes either thought they'd fled or had some other reason not to come after them. What that reason might be, he didn't care to speculate, but he kept the Remington handy. By the time they had all the wiring rigged, the rain had eased off and the clouds had thinned. The gray light of day was fading to evening, their remaining time dwindling fast, when another problem rose up like one of the fish-faced monsters from the depths.

"The lift!" Silas sat down hard and lifted his leg onto the table. "Damn!"

"What about it?" Abigail tried to wipe a gob of tar from her cheek and left a black smear.

"We've got one lift, and two things to lift. Me and the mine."

"Um..." She squinted up at the winch. "Can't it lift both simultaneously?"

"I don't know. The dive suit's about two hundred pounds, I'm another two hundred, and the mine's probably four hundred. *Sea Change* wasn't designed to haul anything so heavy. Eight hundred pounds is almost double what that winch is *supposed* to lift. Once I'm in the water, it'll be fine, but lifting both off the deck..."

"All we can do is try."

Silas squinted at the sky. "We better move *Sea Change* before it gets dark. We'll try it once we get anchored."

"We anchored in the dark before." She argued.

"I know, Abigail, but this time we need to be as close to the wreck as we can manage without dropping our anchor right on it." Silas tried to bite back his temper, but fear, pain, and fatigue swirled in his skull like a hurricane. "Once I'm down there with the mine, I don't want to have to walk too far with my leg."

"Oh." She nodded. "I just...imagine those things coming up while we're getting ready."

"So do I." He imagined a lot worse, tentacled horrors big enough to drag *Sea Change* down to whatever hell lurked within that maelstrom of darkness inside the wreck.

Silas started the engine and laboriously hauled anchor, working the windlass crank with his injured leg propped up on the bow gunnel while Abigail kept them on station. When the anchor cleared the surface, Silas maneuvered close to Devil Reef, using the siren call hammering in his head as much as dead reckoning to gauge their position.

"This is as good as I can guess," he said, handing over the controls to Abigail. "Keep her idling into the wind. When I signal you, shift into neutral."

"Right." Abigail glanced over her shoulder through the cabin to the deck as if suspecting swarms of fish-faced monsters any moment.

Silas lowered the anchor slowly, trying to minimize the noise. The roar of surf on the reef would probably douse the thrum of the engine, but metallic clanks and clatters traveled far underwater. When he felt the tension on the anchor ease, he signaled Abigail and she shifted the boat into neutral. They drifted downwind, and Silas paid out rode. When the yearning call in his head rose to a crescendo, he tied it off. *Sea Change* jerked as the anchor set and their bow came into the wind.

"The sky's starting to clear." Abigail pointed west as he hobbled back into the pilothouse.

"Good. It'll give you some light. The moon should be up soon." He limped aft. "Now, help me with the dive gear."

With his injury, struggling into the dive suit was challenging, slow, painful, and nerve-racking. When they came to the last piece, Silas ran one of his heaviest dock lines through the helmet's lift ring, and then the lift eye on the mine.

"I can cut it free when it's in position and clip the lift line to my helmet."

"And then I winch you up, right?"

"Right." Once inside the wreck, however, Silas doubted he would ever come out again. *Abigail will do the right thing…* "I'll tell you to stop lowering when the mine's just above the seabed. Then you'll have to shift the power transfer lever, and idle *Sea Change* to the left until I'm inside. Then you can just slip the clutch on the lift to drop the mine. You'll have to disconnect the telephone wires and hook up the mine wires to detonate the mine. Just turn the crank hard, like you're making a call, and it should do the job."

"Okay, but…" Abigail glanced between the winch, the pilothouse, and the open engine room hatch. "Too bad we don't have help."

"Well, we can't ask anyone now. You can do it, just one thing at a time."

"Yes, but… I'll have to flip the power transfer lever again to pull you up, and the boat will drift back on the anchor. Won't it pull the wires out or break one of our connections?"

"Damn, you're right." Fatigue, pain, and alcohol were wreaking havoc on his concentration. The answer came easily: idle *Sea Change* into position, lower him and the mine into the wreck, and detonate the mine, but Abigail would never agree to that. When it came to his life or Armageddon, he knew she'd choose the lesser of two evils, but she wouldn't accept a plan to kill him. He thought furiously for some answer she would agree with. *Make something up!* "When the mine's placed, I can drop my weight belt. That'll let me climb the lift line up."

"But without the lift, I won't be able to get you aboard."

Damn it, quit making perfectly sensible arguments! "No, but I can hang onto the air hose while you set off the mine. That'll free the lift line, then I'll tie it around my chest and you lift me up."

"Sounds dangerous."

He barked a laugh. It sounded impossible. "This whole *thing's* dangerous, but—"

Abigail's eyes focused beyond his shoulder and she stabbed a finger to the east. "Silas! Look!"

For a moment Silas feared some monster had risen from Devil Reef, but when he turned, it was only the moon shining from between scudding clouds. But something wasn't right about it. As a sailor, he knew the phases of the moon innately, for the moon governed the tides. It should have been waxing gibbous, but it shone full. *The tides in the canal...they were wrong, too! What the hell?* Then something else caught his eye: the full moon.

"Something's *eating* the moon!"

Chapter Nine

The Deep Gate

It's an eclipse! It's a lunar eclipse, Silas!"

"Impossible! It's not supposed to happen for another week!"

"Another week..." Abigail dashed into the cabin. At the table, she rifled through the tome. "Here! 'When Father Sun and Mother Moon join with the Earth in blood, Father Dagon and Mother Hydra will join in the deep to usher the third of their triune into the world of man.' The moon turns *red* in the shadow of the Earth!"

"Joined in blood..." Silas swallowed hard. "Why didn't you tell me this before?"

"I didn't know what it meant. I didn't think it mattered."

"It matters! The Marshes of Innsmouth formed a...society a long time ago. The Esoteric Order of *Dagon*!"

"I'm sorry, I...just thought it was nonsense."

"But the moon's not *supposed* to be full at all!" Silas hobbled to the table and snatched up his nautical almanac. He flipped to the date and pointed to the entry. "Full in one week."

"Which was the original date of the event in the tome, Silas. They changed the moon to change the date of the event!"

"Changed the *moon*?" He blinked at her. "That's insane!"

She pointed to the moon. "Then explain that!"

Silas cursed and shook his head. “We’re out of time Abigail! Help me with the helmet!”

They muscled the helmet on and dogged down the seals, then Silas hobbled over to sit on the gunnel next to the mine. “Get the hook!” Abigail retrieved the lift hook and he clipped it to the center of the line connecting his helmet to the mine. “Good, now rev up the engine a bit and engage the lift. I’ll close the face plate when I’m up.”

“Right!” Abigail complied, but when she engaged the lift, the engine lugged dangerously with the weight before his feet left the deck.

“Stop!” Silas gritted his teeth. “Rev it up some more and put some slack in the line before you try again.

“Okay.” She revved up the engine just short of full throttle, ran out some line, and threw the lever again.

The engine screamed, then lugged and died.

“Damn it!” Silas untied the line from the helmet to the mine.

“What do we do?” Desperation edged Abigail’s voice like a razor.

“You’ll have to lower me first, then the mine. I’ll push it into the wreck, then drop my belt and climb the rope. It’ll just take longer.” He unclipped the line. “Can you get the engine started?”

“I think so.” Abigail hurried forward, climbed down into the engine room, and grunted with the effort of hauling the crank.

To Silas’s relief, the engine coughed to life. “Now, if we haven’t burned out the clutch…” He checked his light and the big knife at his belt and nodded to Abigail. “Do it. I’ll tell you when I’m on the bottom.” He closed the face plate.

The lift labored, but he rose into the air. Abigail cranked the boom over the sea and lowered him. The ink black water enveloped him in a chill embrace, feet, legs, hips, chest, and finally his head. One last glimpse of the half-eaten moon, and he was under.

“Can you hear me?” Abigail’s voice crackled in his ear.

“Yes.” Silas flipped on the dive light and shone it around. Nothing but blackness surrounded him. The descent seemed to be taking much longer than the first time, until a sudden jolt of pain up his leg as he hit the bottom wrenched a yelp from his throat. “I’m down!” He teetered there for a moment, fighting for balance, then unclipped the line from his helmet. “The line’s free. Take it up and attach it to the mine. Be careful not to tangle the wires!”

“I’ve got it!”

Silas waited. Two eternities passed while he imagined the moon slowly being devoured in shadow. He pointed the light straight up, daring not pan it around for fear of arousing the nest of monsters in the wreck. The yearning hammered at his mind like an echo inside his dive helmet, pulling him, pleading with him to join them. *Come to us! Come home! Join us...* Pain lanced up his leg, snapping his hypnosis, and he realized he'd taken a step toward the wreck, toward oblivion.

"Thank God," he muttered. "Never thought breaking my leg would save my life."

"What's that?" Abigail asked over the phone.

"Nothing. Just talking to myself. How's it going?"

"It's on the way down!"

Silas arched his back to look up. The mine descended out of the murk. When it neared the height of his head, he yelled, "Stop!" into the phone.

The mine stopped at the height of his chest, bobbing up and down with the waves jostling *Sea Change* above. He pushed against it, but it barely moved, and his leg stabbed him with the effort.

"Okay, Abigail, the depth is perfect. Now disengage the power transfer lever, and idle the boat hard over to port, that's *left*. In this wind, she'll swing on the anchor without making any forward headway." Silas didn't even have to look to know what direction the wreck lay in. The call pulled him, pleading with him to join them. He gritted his teeth against the urge. *Oh, I'll join you... I'll send you all straight to hell!*

"Okay. Yell when you're in position. I can barely hear you from forward."

"Okay." Silas waited, and the mine started to drift away. He limped after it, a slow shuffling gait that minimized the strain on his leg. The pain jolted him back toward sanity with every step.

The wreck loomed out of the dark ahead of them, the gaping hole in her side like the maw of some leviathan waiting to swallow him. His calculations had been good: the mine was arcing right toward the gaping hole. In the glare of his light, shapes flicked around inside the ship, dark within dark accented by flecks of silver, luminous eyes reflecting the beam.

The yearning pulled him, and he answered now. *Yes, I'm*

coming... I've got a present for you.

A clawed hand reached over the jagged metal edge, followed by a face. Bulging fish eyes stared at him, the lipless maw opening to reveal rows of needle teeth. Silas's stomach lurched, and he swallowed to keep from vomiting into his helmet. He pointed his powerful light straight into those disconcerting eyes, and the face jerked back out of sight.

They don't like the light... Maybe he could keep them at bay long enough to get the mine placed. "Almost there! Tie off the wheel and get on the lift, Abigail!"

After a short delay, her reply crackled, "Okay! I'm on the lift."

Lurching closer, he strained to shove the mine over the edge, trying to ignore the movement roiling within the deeper darkness, the unblinking eyes, the impossible shapes above, and the deafening call in his skull. The lift rope met with the upper edge of the hole, and the mine swung in. *Thank God the metal's bent inward...*

"Now! Down!" Silas screamed into the phone, but Abigail's reactions weren't so swift this time. *Sea change* continued to drift, the line lifting the mine up. The iron sphere clanged against the edge of the jagged hole, the trailing wires dangerously close to being snagged and severed. Silas couldn't reach the wires, but he could reach the mine and braced his one good leg to push it in as Abigail released the clutch.

As he heaved the mine forward, the light dangled from a lanyard tied to his wrist, sweeping the interior of the wreck. The man-sized creatures shied from the light, but as the mine lowered, the light struck the edge of the jagged hole and shone up overhead. The massive shapes he'd only glimpsed before now became clear: huge ropy arms with clawed tips, pulsing flesh, and plate-sized eyes. As the beam touched one of those huge orbs, the pupil contracted and focused upon him.

Terror unlike anything he'd ever felt lanced through him. A low wail of woe echoed within his helmet, his own voice. Then another voice reverberated through his head, hammering at his skull.

Join us, Silas Marsh! Your only future lies with us. The voice washed away his fear, his confusion, and his will.

Yes... Silas started to crawl over the jagged edge, but a four hundred pound sphere of iron clanged against his helmet, ringing even louder than the yearning call. Sanity…solidity…and the stabbing pain of his leg vied against the compulsion. He slammed his shoulder into the massive iron sphere, driving it into the hole as the lift line paid out. But as the mine screeched against the bent teeth of the ruined hull to settle down in its final grave, clawed hands reached around it to grasp him. One caught the wire and it came dangerously taut.

"NO!" Silas shone his light in their faces, reaching for the heavy knife at his belt. The fishy figures reeled back, cringing away, but others swam forth, claws reaching for him.

"What?" Abigail cried. "What's happening!"

"They're all over the damned place! They're on me!" He slashed at the scrabbling hands, the gnashing teeth. Black blood darkened the water, but there were too many. Claws raked the heavy canvas of his suit, unable to penetrate, but dragging him in while the yearning call hammered at his fragile will. There was only one answer, one refuge where they couldn't reach him. "Trigger the mine! Do it, Abigail, before it's too late!"

"No!" her voice crackled, edged with panic. "Unclip your weights and climb! I won't kill you!"

"Blow it, Abigail, or you'll kill *everyone*!" A lurid face lunged at his faceplate, jaws gaping, but Silas filled that maw with his knife, driving the tip deep. The teeth came down on his wrist, and pinholes of wetness dampened his forearm. Hands grasped, pulling him over the ragged edge of the hole. His leg struck something and he screamed.

"Silas! Your weight belt! Don't make me do this! I can't!"

He slashed madly, releasing the light and scrabbling desperately to his feet. The agony of his leg stabbed his every movement, jerking him back to reality, away from the irresistible call. The creatures had released him but swam in a mass just out of reach. The knife had taught them fear, and they hated the light. Thankfully, they seemed to be ignoring the mine. *Maybe…maybe I've got a chance.*

But as Silas reached for the clip holding his weight belt, another light filled the wreck's hold. A sickly yellow illumination shone from the depths of the maelstrom of darkness swirling above him. At its core, a space yawned open, widening like a mouth that would swallow the world. Within, beyond that pit of blackness, a city, a world, and a monstrosity that defied sanity swelled into view. The city from his nightmares, impossible structures, improbable angles, and hundreds…no *thousands* of hellish shapes skittering about like maggots and beetles and flies swarming a rotting corpse. And above it loomed an unimaginable shape, writhing tentacles amid a bulbous head, wings that spanned the sky like the coming of night, clawed hands that could crush ships.

The deep gate… The prophecy of Abigail's tome, the end of the world of man, reached forth.

Silas's numb fingers found the clip to his weight belt and pulled. His feet left the twisted tangle of steel and he rose up, but his nightmares would not let him go so easily. The fishy shapes swarmed in on him, scrabbling and biting, dragging and clawing. One caught the lantern and pulled so hard the lanyard snapped. The light spun away. He screamed and slashed, fumbling through the mass of shapes to find the lift line, knowing he couldn't, knowing he would fail. Abigail wouldn't trigger the mine, and that impossibility of madness would claw through the hole in creation to consume the Earth.

"Do it, Abigail!" Amid the writhing and gnashing scaled flesh, Silas's free hand found a taut rope. He clenched it and pulled, catching a glimpse of open water outside the ship.

"No! Climb, Silas! You can do it! The moon's not red yet! You have time!"

"They're on me! I can't fight and climb." His light flickered among the writhing shapes.

"Silas! Cut the…" Her words ended in static.

"What?" He slashed and stabbed blindly, trying to climb one-handed. He couldn't drop the knife with so many of them on him. They'd drag him back inside.

"I said…the air…bubbles will…and climb!"

Bubbles? Of course. Silas stabbed over his shoulder with the heavy knife and felt for the air hose. One slash opened it, blasting compressed air into the wrecked ship and enveloping him in a cloud of bubbles. The valve that kept the sea from rushing in through the severed hose clacked closed, and the grasping hands and gnashing teeth fell away.

Free…I'm free. With the voices of a thousand monsters

yammering in his mind, Silas Marsh renounced his life, his family, and the siren call. *Survive! I can survive this!* He dropped his knife and climbed madly for the surface.

"I'm free, Abigail! I'm climbing!"

But he received no answer, nothing but static.

Probably cut the phone line with the air hose. He dragged himself up hand over hand, going by feel in the faint light of the waning moon gleaming down through the water.

Abigail would be frantically changing the phone wires to the detonation circuit, her hand hovering over the crank that would send a jolt of electricity down the cables to blast the wreck, the monsters, and that vile hole in reality straight to hell.

Do it! Do it now, before it's too late! No mine, no explosive or bomb made by mankind could harm that monstrosity beyond the portal. If it gained purchase in this world, it would end mankind as a man might end a colony of ants.

Silas…come back…come home…

His ears popped as pressure eased, then pain lanced through his leg and his grip slid back on the rope. Silas twisted and looked down through the side port of his helmet and wished he hadn't. Through the cloud of bubbles, the light from inside the wreck illuminated a mass of fishy shapes boiling from the jagged hole. They swam up to grasp him, to drag him down. One had hold of his broken leg, its grip sending lightning bolts of pain through him. Teeth clamped on his thigh, moisture seeping in through the holes in the heavy canvas. Water trickled down his leg, filling his boot and weighing him down. He clubbed the thing with a fist, gouging at its bulbous eyes. It released him, and he got a few more precious handholds before the next one reached him.

Claws scratched at the canvas of his suit, scrabbling up his back, trying to pull him off the rope. A lurid face peered at him through the side port of his helmet, webbed fingers scrabbling at the wing nuts that held the glass in place. Bronze squeaked as one of the nuts began to turn.

No, no, no! Not now! Not when I've got a chance…

Silas freed one hand and grasped the fishy throat. With the grip of a sailor fortified by panic, Silas squeezed. The toothy mouth gaped, clawed hands grasping at his wrist as fragile bones crunched under his fingers. A hoarse scream reached his ears as the grip on his wrist weakened. The scream, he realized, was his.

Releasing his grasp, he climbed frantically. The fading light of the moon overhead shifted from silvery to the hue of dried blood. It was time. A subsonic thrum of energy began to sing along his bones. The deep gate was opening, and Silas envisioned the great clawed hand reaching through from beyond. The surface loomed just overhead, but even as he broke through the undulating mirror, another clawed hand closed on his broken leg.

Silas...come back to us...

Agony shot through him in torrents as the ends of fractured bone grated through tortured muscle. His grip on the rope slipped, but he fought upward, reaching through to the world of air, the world of man. He caught a glimpse of Abigail at the rail of *Sea Change* grasping the phone box in one arm, her hand on the crank, eyes impossibly wide, and her face pale with panic. A sanguineous moon shone down from the sky, Father Sun, Mother Moon, and the Earth joined in blood.

A webbed hand reached over Silas's shoulder, claws grating against his faceplate. Gold glinted on one of the digits, a ring grown over by the membranous webbing, three familiar braided strands of tarnished gold.

Silas, my boy...come home... The call beat on his mind like a hammer on fragile glass.

Oh, God, no...not that...please no... Silas reached up and grasped the rope higher, pulling with his last ounce of strength.

"*Do it*!" he screamed, praying to God that Abigail would hear him.

Between the clawed fingers obscuring his view, past the glint of the ring, Silas saw Abigail crank the handle. He wrapped an arm around the suddenly slack lift line in one last desperate grasp for survival.

A pressure wave slammed into Silas like a runaway train, wrenching muscles and cracking joints. His head slammed against the back of his helmet, shooting stars through his brain. The creature's grip on him loosed as he was thrown. Then something slapped him in the chest, and his forehead clanged against the faceplate.

Silas wondered, as darkness closed over him, why the moon tasted like blood.

Epilogue

At Sea

Silas woke to the familiar thrum of *Sea Change*'s engine vibrating through his head and the taste of blood in his mouth. There was pain, too, and plenty of it, but he was breathing, and therefore alive. *Death wouldn't hurt like this.*

He blinked his one good eye open and wondered if he was blind for a moment, but then moonlight, silvery and clear, swept into view. The roll of the deck and the pitch of the engine told him *Sea Change* was underway, and at sea. He was lying on his back on deck, still in his dive gear except for the helmet.

He worked his tongue around in his mouth and found a split lip, a newly chipped tooth, and a good bit of blood. He reached up to touch his pounding forehead and felt a lump there the size of a goose egg. He had a similar one on the back of his head, and his neck ached. *Rattled around inside the dive helmet like a bean in a cup…* He closed his eye and saw again the three braided strands of gold, his mother's wedding ring on the webbed hand of that monster.

He closed his eye and prayed. *They're dead. Please, God, let them be dead.* He dragged in a breath, the faint siren call still ringing in his mind. His prayer, it seemed, would not be answered.

Silas tried to sit up and failed, but he managed to roll over. His leg stabbed him, but it seemed still attached, which was more than he'd expected. He forced himself up to hands and knees and felt every muscle protest.

"You're alive!"

"Sort of." Silas glanced up through the cabin to the pilothouse to see Abigail at the wheel.

She grinned at him. "You may want to come up here and steer if you can manage it. I have no idea where we are!"

He glanced around and caught a glimpse of Innsmouth light about a mile behind them. Still on all fours, he leaned over the gunnel and peered forward. They topped a swell, and he caught a glimpse of the Plum Island Sound sea buoy.

"Steer ten more degrees to port. We should be clear of the shoals already."

"Okay." She turned the wheel and *Sea Change* answered. "How do you feel?"

"Like I've been chewed up and spat out, then stomped on for good measure!" Yelling hurt his head. He looked around the deck and spotted the dive helmet. The lift line was looped under his arms and tied in an incomprehensible knot. "How did you get me aboard?"

"You were just floating there, so I hooked the lift line with that pole thingamabob, and tied a knot. Easy as pie!" She seemed positively ebullient. "I didn't want to just sit there over the wreck, but I couldn't hoist the anchor, so I cut it loose. Sorry."

"Don't be." Silas didn't want to be anywhere near Devil Reef either.

Gritting bloody teeth, he managed to push himself up on one good leg, discovering dozens of new aches and pains. He sat on the dormant air compressor, and worked at the suit's seals, finally freeing himself of its clammy embrace. The air felt good against his skin again. He hobbled into the cabin and retrieved the bottle from the cupboard. There were perhaps two good swallows left. He limped forward and stepped into the pilothouse.

"Breakfast?" He held out the bottle to Abigail.

"On an empty stomach?" She grimaced. "No thanks. I'd be sick."

"Coffee then?" He pulled the cork and upended the last of the bottle, swallowing twice. The alcohol stung his cut lip, but the taste of blood vanished in the burning glory of Canadian whiskey.

"I'd love a cup, and maybe something to eat if there is anything."

"Coffee and crackers is the best I can do." He turned back to the cabin.

"Sorry I nearly killed you, by the way," she called over her shoulder.

"What?" Silas blinked back at her in shock. "You're the only reason I'm still breathing, Abigail. You should have blown it earlier. Those things could have pulled the wires from the mine at any moment."

"Yes, well, I couldn't, and they didn't." She sounded a little hurt, and he realized how ungrateful he was being.

"But thank you for risking the entire world to save my life."

"You're welcome." She flashed him a smile and turned back to the wheel.

As he started making coffee, the siren song hummed in the back of his mind. The power of that call seemed lesser now, although it was still there. He didn't have to ask Abigail what had happened to the creature that had been trying to drag him down at that last moment. The persistent, familiar call to come home told him she had survived. He hobbled forward again, grabbing a box of crackers on the way, and tossed them on the console.

"I'd say it feels good to be alive, but I hurt all over." He leaned back with a wince.

"We *are* alive!" Abigail took a cracker and nibbled it. "We *beat* them, Silas! We outfoxed those hideous people in Innsmouth, we stopped this…*thing* from happening, and we even saved ourselves in the process!"

"Well, we sure as hell won a battle, but…" Silas looked over his shoulder. Devil Reef was far behind them now, out of sight, but the yearning remained.

"But what?" She looked at him sidelong. "You don't seem very happy."

"Oh, I'm happy to be alive, but…" He looked over his shoulder again. *I'll be doing that for the rest of my life, I suppose.* "I… saw things down there, Abigail. Things that shouldn't be, but are. Things that…*can't* exist, but do."

"But we blew them up! That blast…" She shook her head. "Well, you should have *seen* it. I wonder how you survived, really. Nothing down there could have survived that!"

Silas wondered if she was right, prayed so, but honestly didn't know if things like what he'd seen through that portal *could* be killed. And if they couldn't, they would try again, another time, another place; when and where, there was no way to know. "Maybe… I don't know whether you *can* win against things like that."

"Take the wheel. I want to show you something."

"All right." Silas edged past her, embarrassed for the first time about his condition, bloody, pants soaked, one boot, shirt torn. "Grab a clean shirt from the fo'c'sle, too, please."

"Sure."

Abigail went below for a bit, and Silas adjusted course minutely out of habit. They'd be in Annisquam before sunup, so he throttled back some. *Better to take the channel in daylight on a rising tide.*

"Here." Abigail held out a flannel shirt as she stepped back up into the pilothouse. Under her arm, she held the old tome that had set them on this crazy adventure to begin with.

"Thanks." Silas struggled into the clean shirt, the muscles of his back and shoulders protesting with every move.

"So, look here, Mister *Can't Win*." She flipped to the familiar page with the coordinates of Devil Reef, and pointed to the passage. "Look."

Silas peered down in the wavering lamplight and gaped. The celestial fixes, and the date and time of the event were gone. There was a gap in the text. The rest of the page remained, the lurid illustrations in the margins, but the details were blank.

"And here!" She turned to the page with the impossible city he'd seen both in his nightmares and through the portal within the wreck.

The entire page was blank.

"Well, I'll be damned." A weight lifted off Silas's aching shoulders.

"You see? We really did win." She closed the book and put it on the console. "As improbable as it sounds, we saved the world. Cheer up, sourpuss!"

"Sorry." He smiled at her, but it felt forced and his lip hurt. "I hit my head pretty hard. I guess I'm still not thinking straight."

"Oh, you really should sit and put your leg up." She nodded to the wheel. "I can steer. I'm getting pretty good at it! You've made a sailor out of a librarian, Silas!"

That brought a more genuine smile. "Okay, Able Seaman Foreman, steer about ten degrees to port of the lighthouse until you see the Annisquam sea buoy, then give me a yell."

"Aye aye, Captain!" She sketched a snappy salute and slipped past him to take the wheel. "And I would take a cup of that coffee, if you can manage it."

"Be a few minutes." Silas limped back into the cabin, sat at the chart table and put his leg up. The swelling had increased again with all the walking. He watched the pot on the stove, willing it to boil.

"So, what do you plan to do now?" Abigail asked over her shoulder.

"Do?" He frowned and considered the question seriously. Could he go back to just fishing, running lobster pots, doing salvage and deliveries to the islands? Yes, fishing and running his boat...that he could do, but he'd probably sell his dive gear. "Get *Sea Change* fixed up, buy a new anchor, and keep doing what I've always done, I guess."

"You don't think your family will press charges for stealing the mine and damaging their boat?"

"Oh, the Marsh family doesn't go in much for calling the coppers, and I'll never set foot in Innsmouth again. If they come looking for me in Kingsport, well..." He shrugged and rubbed his eye, wondering if time would make him a liar. "What about you, Abigail? You're going back to the library, right?"

"Oh, of course!"

"No more magical tomes or adventures?"

"Ha! Not on your *life*, Silas Marsh!" She grinned back at him. "I think I'll stick to reading novels from now on, go see a picture show now and then, or maybe a play. There's a new production in town, you know. *The King in Yellow*. It's supposed to be quite scandalous! Maybe when you get out of the hospital, you'd go see it with me?"

Surprised at her forward question, he thought about it, about Abigail. *A sailor and a university librarian?* Silas shook his head with a smile; he admired Abigail's spunk, but they were too different. Their lives would mix like oil and water. "Sorry, but picture shows and plays aren't really my cup of java."

"Suit yourself." She turned back to the wheel. "There's more to life than fishing and boats, you know."

"Perhaps, but..." Silas looked out over the turbulent ocean. His mother's call echoed faintly in his mind, and he knew he couldn't resist it forever. "I belong to the sea. It's in my blood."

About the Author

The Deep Gate represents two firsts in Chris A. Jackson's writing career: it is his first contemporary sea story, as well as his first work of horror. The former wasn't a difficult venture, for as the son of a commercial fisherman with more than forty years of sea experience, writing about it came naturally. The only difficulty was holding back on the nautical jargon, which can be as alien to the nautically uninitiated as *Prophesiae Profana* was to Silas Marsh. As for the horror elements, Chris had the advantage of playing and enjoying the *Arkham Horror* game, but also relied heavily upon input from his wife Anne, a life-long fan of the genre and Lovecraft's Mythos to boot. Chris and his wife have co-authored several novels together, so joining forces on this novella also came naturally, with little added marital stress.

Chris's other works include award-winning novels of nautical fantasy, high fantasy, and contemporary fantasy. He has also written numerous RPG tie-in stories for several different gaming companies and third-party publishers, including Paizo Publishing's Pathfinder Tales, Catalyst Game Labs' Shadowrun anthologies, and Privateer Press's Iron Kingdoms.

Chris and Anne currently spend their summers in the Smoky Mountains of North Carolina and winters aboard their beloved sailboat, *Mr. Mac*, in the Caribbean. For more about Chris's writing, including free sample chapters of much of his work, visit jaxbooks.com. If you want to see what sailing the Caribbean is really like, visit their sailing blog at www.sailmrmac.blogspot.com

Harken to me! The Age of Man shall see twilight, and night shall forever reign in the New Age! Ye faithless be aware! In the twenty-sixth year of the twentieth century from the birth of the prophet of Christendom, on the nineteenth day of the sixth month shall begin the New Age. The reckoning will come, and all who do not throw down their false gods and kneel shall be consumed. On this day shall the Deep Gate open between R'lyeh and the temple of the True Disciples. Look unto the stars that ye may know and witness the glorious reunification of the triune of star travelers!

Altair, 25° 58' 02 14h 32s

Jove, 47° 32' 02 14h 32s

As Father Sun and Mother Moon join with the Earth in blood, Father Dagon and Mother Hydra will join in the deep to usher the third of their triune into the world of Man. And lo, the three shall be as One and rule eternity over the world of mankind. When the Triune shall unite, and three become One, the True Disciples shall rise from the sea in flood and flow across the land unto the mountains, slaying the unbelievers, consuming their flesh, and purifying the land with their blood. All the works of Man shall be cast down, their heathen beliefs drowned beneath waves of vengeance. Only the chosen of the Disciples shall be spared, and the get of their loins shall be the Redeemed. Baptized in the waves, they shall serve in eternal life within the darkness of their lord, the One! Thus shall end the Age of Man and begin the glorious era of the Elder Gods.

- Prior to the change from Julian calendar to Gregorian, the new year started in March, not January. Translate the date. *Cripes! That's next week!
- "R'lyeh"? No translation from Latin.
  - Check world atlas.
- What might the term "star travelers" refer to?
- Jove is Jupiter, and Altair is a star. What do these numbers signify? Ask Professor Withers.
- Are these the names of ancient gods or mythological beings? Which civilization? Check with Professor Félix.

5829-29:17

MARINE DETECTION STATION,

NAHANT, MASSACHUSETTS

September 18, 1926

From: Commanding officer, US Naval Experimental Sub-marine Detection Division

To: Commandant, Charlestown Naval Yard, Charlestown, Massachusetts

Subject: Sonic detection of marine detonation.

Enclosures: Sonographic recording of anomaly dated September 16, 1926
Mark 5 Sea Mine schematics.

Capt. William M. Crane, Commandant,

At 0025 hours local, the US Naval Experimental Sub-marine Detection Station recorded an underwater sonic anomaly northeast of its Cape Ann hydrographic listening installation. Analysis by station staff immediately determined this anomaly to be a sub-marine explosion consistent with the detonation of a Mark 5 sea mine. Although the signal was confounded by high sea and surf noise conditions, the signature of the blast was unmistakable. The distance of the blast was estimated at no more than 15 nautical miles from hydrophone placement, and the direction of the explosion within sixty degrees of north. Due to the incomplete recovery of more than ten thousand sea mines deployed off New England during the Great War, the possibility of an unrecovered sea mine being broken loose from its mooring in the high sea conditions of the ongoing north-easterly storm seems the most likely explanation.

Although only one explosion was detected, the risk of additional sea mines being broken loose by the storm conditions has prompted me to recommend a notice to mariners be published and posted at Kingsport, Gloucester, Annisquam, Innsmouth, and Newburyport harbors, and US Coast Guard be notified as to the possibility of other floating explosive hazards. Sparse marine traffic in the area during the recent inclement weather has decreased the risk of shipping hazards, but the subsequent risk is deemed significant. Collision of commercial fishing or merchant marine vessel with a Mark 5 sea mine would be catastrophic, risking numerous human lives.

Notice to mariners and US Coast Guard should include a warning about proper disposal of unexploded ordinance, precautions to be taken, and notification of US Naval Command. If additional sea mines are found floating free in coastal waters, the deployment of a US Navy minesweeping vessel should be considered.

1104

It should also be noted that, without the continuance of the threate
Experimental Sub-marine Detection Division, this potential threat to
mariners would have gone unnoticed. This alone should be sufficient
to justify the continuance of our meager budget. The advance of
hydrophone technology, and the protection of our country, is depende
on our continued research and development efforts.

Sincerely,

Harold Fishburne

Harrold Fishburne
Lt. Commander USN
US Naval Experimen...

IN REPLY ADDRESS
COMMANDER OF CNS
AND REFER TO NO.
1077-43:64

CHARLESTOWN NAVAL YARD,
CHARLESTOWN, MASSACHUSETTS

September 19, 1926

From: Commandant, Charlestown Naval Yard
To: Commanding officer, US Naval Experimental Sub-marine Detection Division

Subject: Reply to your request of Sept. 18.

Harry,

I can't blame you for trying, but this fish won't swim with me. I'll send your request for a notice to mariners to the Coast Guard commandant, but don't expect me to go to bat for your funding. If you want to keep listening for fish farts, you'll have to do it on your own nickel. One unexploded mine isn't a threat to our nation, or even merchant shipping. If some fisherman blows himself to bits messing with a Mark 5, let the Coast Guard pick up the pieces.

Also, I know damn well what a Mark 5 looks like, and don't presume to tell me how to deploy my resources. A minesweeper is out of the question. We'll leave this up to the Coasties. They've got to do something to earn their pay besides beachcombing for wreckage.

If your funding doesn't come through, let me know. I could use another yard officer. Post-war budget cuts have put all our jobs on the chopping block.

Give my best to Betty and the kids.

Sincerely,

William M. Crane

William M. Crane
Captain, USN
Commandant, Charlestown Naval Yard,
Charlestown, Massachusetts

10813

Notes on Devil Reef—

From offshore, watch for breaking water southeast of the hill on Plum Island. Approach in calm weather only, high tide, never on a new moon! There's a shallow cut between the foul ground of Plum Island and Devil Reef, but only navigable at high tide in calm weather. Very good fishing between Plum Island and Devil Reef, and you're out of sight of Innsmouth, so not likely to get run off by the Marshes. If you see a boat coming out from Innsmouth, haul anchor and haul ass! The Marshes do NOT like anyone in this area. Traps or longlines left here will be cut. From inshore, about 300 yards east of Red 8A, there is a cut to the north. Watch the shallows east of 8A, keep them to port. Should be ten feet of water at low there, deepening to 20 as you make your way north. Keep close to the shoal to starboard, visible at low water. When the shoal to the east deepens, you can turn northeast into deeper water and anchor. Devil Reef is clearly visible at low water, and breaks even in low swells. Don't venture too close, especially if the surf is up. There is foul ground not marked on the chart near the reef, and anchors have been lost due to snagging. There's also a lot of lost fishing gear littering the bottom here, from cut buoys and fouled gear. Fishing here is very good, but in clear weather you'll get a visit from Innsmouth in short order. Be prepared to haul anchor and scoot. In very calm weather, you can escape this deep inlet to the northwest between Devil Reef and Plum Island, but watch for breakers on both sides. Do not attempt this cut in heavy seas. You can come and go in the dark easily enough, and a night's catch can make your trip, but never on the new moon!

Good fishing
Out of sight
of town.
Devil Reef
Breakers
Foul
Kelp
Bass Rock
Shoaling,
Keep buoy to North!
Buoy moved '25
Innsmouth Light
6s 80ft
SHIFTING
CHANNEL
STEEP HILL
INNSMOUTH BEACH
W
S.E
S.W
S

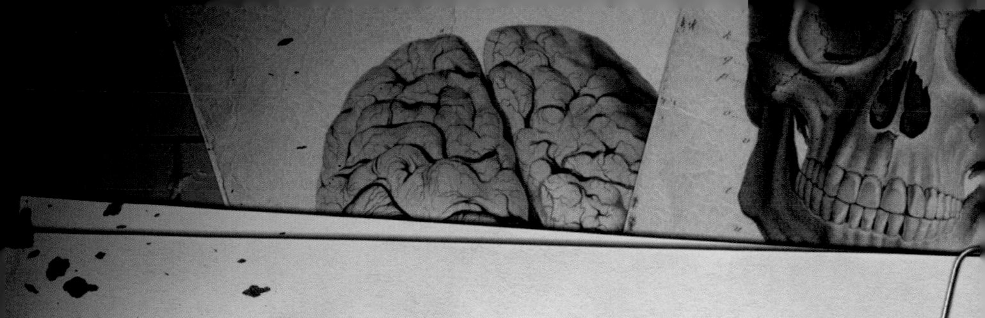

ST. MARY'S HOSPITAL TRAUMA DEPARTMENT, ARKHAM, MASSACHUSETTS

MEDICAL REPORT

Patient name: Silas Marsh
Sex: Male
Date of Birth: 10/14/1890
Weight: 195 pounds Height: 6' 2"
Date of Arrival: September 16, 1926 Time of Arrival: 3:45 PM
Condition: Multiple trauma to head, leg, arms, and face. Fractured fibula, probable concussion, alcohol intoxication.
Prognosis: Good. Held for observation due to probable concussion, the diagnosis of which was confounded by alcohol.

Physician's Notes:
The patient arrived in the company of a young woman who said she found him in an alley off of River Street in Arkham that afternoon. She seemed respectable, stated that she "Didn't want to get involved in any trouble," and left the hospital. The patient was lucid, ambulatory with aid, showing signs of mild confusion and pain, and smelled of distilled spirits. He stated that he was a sailor who was in town up from Kingsport due to the recent inclement weather, and he claimed that he was beaten and robbed while walking the wharves along the river. This is not an uncommon occurrence in that area of town, and the medical staff found no reason to doubt his story.

The patient's single pupil (his left eye is missing due to a previous trauma) was responsive, but somewhat sluggish. Injuries included a fractured left fibula, extensive bruising on his back, arms, and legs, facial lacerations, and a head wound consistent with the impact of a blunt object. The patient stated that he was hit from behind and briefly lost consciousness. The head wound was not depressed, although the skin was split. These injuries are consistent with the patient's claim of being beaten, but there were curiously no injuries to ribs or abdomen, which are often found when a victim is beaten. His knuckles were skinned, suggesting that he fought his attackers, and there were minor lacerations on forearms suggestive of defensive wounds, including several small puncture wounds, the origin of which remained undetermined. The pattern and number of injuries suggests at least two, possibly more attackers.

The patient knew his name, the date, and where he was. He remained conscious while his broken leg was set, despite this physician's refusal to provide morphine for pain. The choice to give no morphine was due to head trauma and the potential for alcohol in the patient's bloodstream. The patient was cooperative and not violent, although his cursing during the treatment of his leg and stitching of his head wound was loud and inventive. After the fracture was stabilized, a cast of plaster of Paris was applied from knee to toes. He seemed giddy at times, even breaking into laughter at no provocation more than once—further indicating possible alcohol intoxication—yet he appeared to be reasonably unimpaired. The nursing staff reported him in high spirits, amiable, and very friendly. Although the patient wished to leave after his cast was set, he was held for observation due to possible concussion, which was difficult to diagnose while alcohol remained in his system. He claimed that he did not see his attackers and did not want a police report filed. A letter will be sent to the Miskatonic County Sheriff's Office as well as the Arkham City Police Department outlining this occurrence, but the patient's name will be withheld. Another letter will be sent to the Arkham Advertiser of the occurrence recommending that a general word of caution be published in the newspaper under the interest of public safety. The mention of multiple attackers was stressed in all of these communications.

Signed:

Doctor Anthony Forscythe, Director of
Trauma Medicine, St. Mary's Hospital,
Arkham, Massachusetts.

Addendum, September 17, 1926
The patient Silas Marsh departed the hospital prior to discharge early this morning AMA. The nursing staff stated that they tried to stop him, but he insisted upon leaving. He left St. Mary's Hospital at approximately 6AM under his own power.

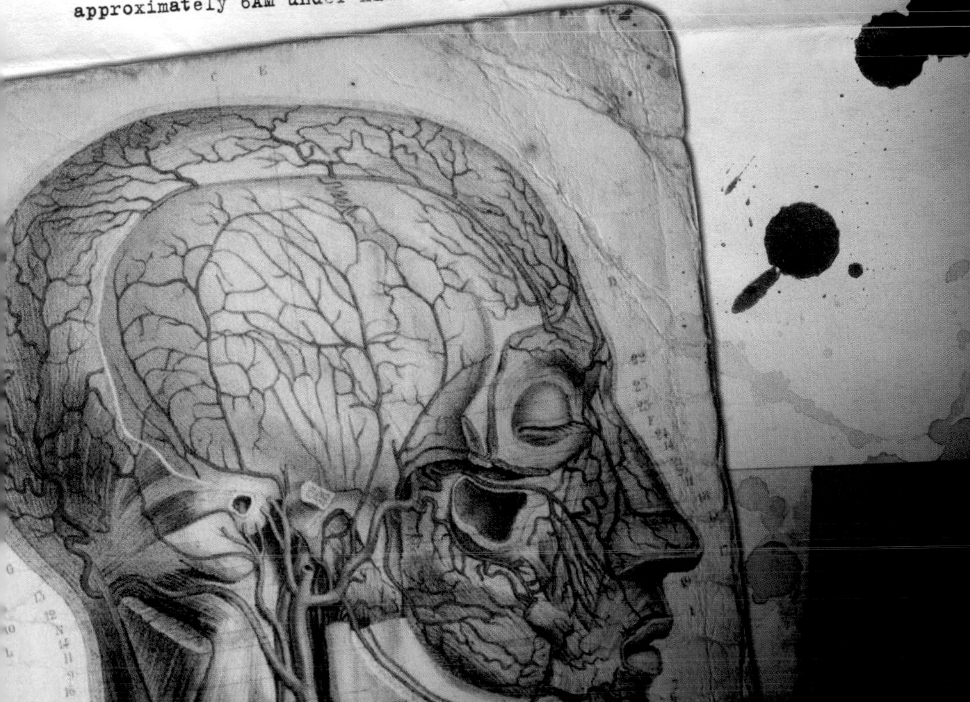

Office of the Librarian
Orne Library
Miskatonic University, Arkham, Massachusetts

September 20, 1926

To: Dean of the College of Arts and Sciences, Miskatonic University
From: Head Librarian, Orne Library, Miskatonic University

Subject: Letter of Reprimand for Abigail Foreman, Librarian

Dear Dean Nelson,

It is with much regret that I find it necessary to tender this letter of reprimand for your approval. Let it be stressed that, to date, Miss Abigail Foreman, Librarian of seven years and supervisor of Orne Library's Restricted Section, has been an exemplary employee of the university. She has always been conscientious, punctual, diligent, and mindful of her duties. This unfortunate incident is the first on her record.

On the date of September 17th, Miss Foreman reported to the library exceedingly late and in a state of upset and dishevelment. She had taken the previous day off, citing a family emergency, and, unbeknownst to the library staff at the time, had taken a single book from the Restricted Section with her. Although it is no[t] against library policy for materials of the Restricted Section to be removed from the library, to do so requires a signature from the Head Librarian (myself), and a signed release form. Miss Forem[an] did neither of these necessary steps of our standard protocol, and what is far worse, returned the priceless book to the library damaged beyond repair.

Although largely intact, the book in question, a sixteenth-centu[ry] hand printed and illustrated tome entitled Prophesiae Profana, the work of a defrocked Roman Catholic monk, had minor water damage and one passage of text, and one whole-page illustration that appeared to have been removed or erased by some unknown, possibly chemical, means. The passage was in a section of the te[xt] a prophecy, referring to an event of biblical proportions that wa[s] supposed to end the world. Although copies of this text have be[en] made over the years, and the text itself was copied from a mu older tome of Mesopotamian origin, the damage to this priceless artifact cannot be ignored. Miss Foreman was apologetic for the damage done to the text, but insisted that the tome did not leave her possession, and that she did not in any way intentionally damage the pages. She remained adamant in her assertion even when faced with the evidence of the damage done.

Repair of the damage done to the tome is impossible, and the value of the tome still remains considerable, as it is both irreplaceable and unique. I plan to personally requisition a copy to be made of the missing text from another source, and attach an addendum to the tome for future researchers. Prophesiae Profana has been returned to the Restricted Section, and Miss Foreman has been reassigned to care for the library's more mundane collections. It is my feeling that her employment with the university should not be terminated, and that her reassignment and this letter of reprimand be her only censure.

It is of note that Miss Foreman was seen in the company of a rather rough fellow of questionable repute on the day prior to her absence. When asked whether this man might have been responsible for the damage to Prophesiae Profana, Miss Foreman became visibly agitated, refused to give his name, and insisted that he was in her employ at the recommendation of Professor Withers of the Science Department. When asked what type of service she had employed this man to perform, Miss Foreman stated that he was a mariner skilled in celestial navigation, and she paid him ten dollars to translate celestial data in Prophesiae Profana into terrestrial locations. Dr. Withers corroborated Miss Foreman's claim, stating that he was too busy to personally help her, and suggested she find someone skilled in celestial navigation. Although this man may be the one responsible for the damage to Prophesiae Profana, without testimony by Miss Foreman or evidence to prove his guilt, pressing charges would be a fruitless effort.

Sincerely,
Professor Henry Armitage,
Head Librarian, Orne Library,
Miskatonic University.

EXPLANATIONS OF VARIANCES IN LUNAR ORBIT OF SEPTEMBER, 1926

Professor Norman Withers

Miskatonic University, Arkham, Massachusetts

Submitted for publication to
Astronomical Journal
Benjamin Boss, Editor

ABSTRACT:

On the dates of September 14-16, 1926, six sudden and unprecedented changes in the orbit of the Moon were independently observed and documented by numerous astronomers and amateur star-gazers around the world (Ref. 1,2,4,8). This anomaly was first observed at the Royal Observatory Greenwich by the eminent Scottish astronomer, Professor John Jackson. Communications via telegraph and wireless radio quickly confirmed independent observations of this phenomenon, which was in turn verified by changes in tidal variations, and the subsequent event of an untimely lunar eclipse on the night of September 16 before reverting, equally inexplicably, to its original course. These facts are incontrovertible, and will not be discussed in this article. The short duration and utterly unexpected nature of the event precluded a statistically significant number of precise observations of the phenomenon. This researcher's aim is to hypothesize on the phenomenon that might have caused this unprecedented and near-biblical event.

HYPOTHESIS ONE: Transit of the Solar System by an extrasolar body.
Extrasolar astronomical bodies have been previously hypothesized, but not directly observed or verified by orbital variations of solar bodies (Ref. 5, 7). A planetoid-sized extrasolar mass of approximately 0.05 Earth Mass, or 6×10^{20} kg, could theoretically pass in a parabolic orbit of the Earth and thus perturb the orbit of the Moon incrementally. This theory is mathematically sound (Ref. 12, 14) but problematic in that the body's passage would also alter the orbit of the Earth itself. No such corroborating orbital variations in the Earth's orbit, measurable by angular observations of other planets and astronomical bodies, has occurred (Ref. 9, 10), but the hypothesis cannot be ruled out with current data. Numerous observations of the heavens were conducted by this researcher and other reputable astronomers around the world, and no unexpected planetary or asteroidal bodies were discovered (Ref. 7, 8).

HYPOTHESIS TWO: Solar magnetic effect.
The magnetism of the Earth is well documented (Ref. 6) and the iron-base of its core hypothesized (Ref. 8). If the iron core

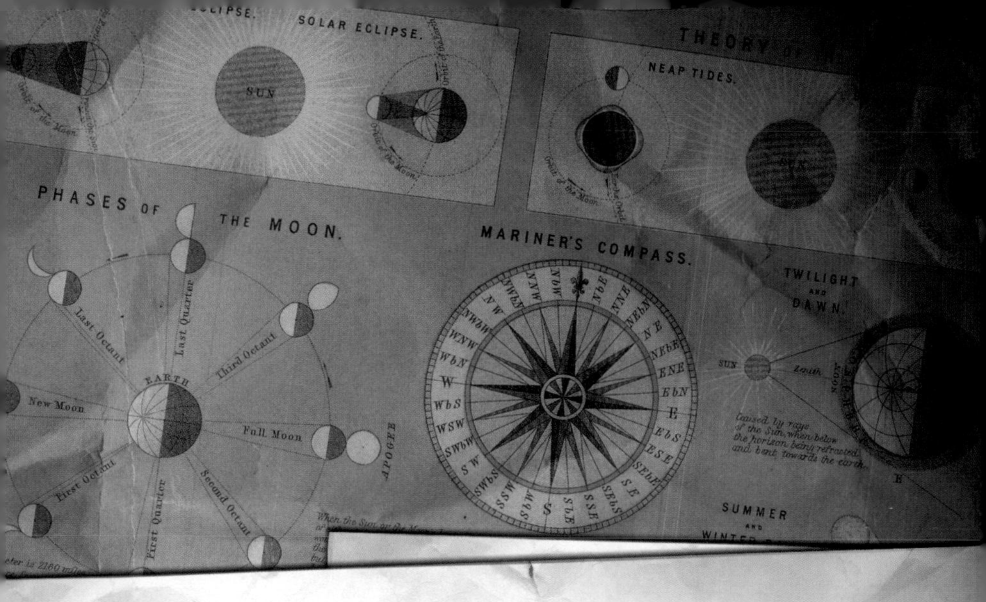

hypothesis is correct, magnetic effects on a solar system-wide scale could result in perturbations of the orbits of planetary bodies. It has been theorized by other researchers (Ref. 13) that the Moon is made up of largely igneous rock, and low in iron content. This disparity in makeup would allow for a disparity in the effect of powerful magnetic effects between the Earth and the Moon. Solar events, or "storms" have been hypothesized to generate exactly such magnetic anomalies (Ref. 12). Sequential waves of magnetic energy from the Sun could generate numerous similar variations in orbital relationships between the Earth and her moon. Such global magnetic effects might not be detectable by instrumentation we possess.

HYPOTHESIS THREE: Lunar asteroidal impacts.
Telescopic observations of the lunar surface show great remnants of large asteroidal impacts in the form of craters (Ref. 9, 15). It would be naïve to assume that such asteroidal impacts are only historical, and not an ongoing phenomenon. Additionally, since the Moon is in one-to-one spin-orbit coupling, we have no notion of what might be occurring on its far side. We hypothesize that sequential large asteroidal impacts on the far side of the Moon could perturb its orbital path. The impact masses would have to range from 10^{13}, to 10^{15} kg (see figure 3). The Earth's atmosphere would offer us some protection from such impacts, but the threat of asteroidal impacts is quite real, as is evidenced by the craters in New Mexico and Western Australia. A confounding lack of observation of asteroidal activity in our atmosphere is noted.

HYPOTHESIS FOUR: Unknown gravitational anomalies.
Gravitational theory is ever evolving, as we see by the recent introduction of Albert Einstein's recent general theory of relativity. Solar system-wide gravitational effects may not be detectable with our current instrumentation due to the well-established equivalence principal (Ref. 13). Could not a gravitational force disparately affect the Moon and the Earth? Our knowledge of gravitational effects on astronomical bodies is growing, but is still in its infancy.

PAGE 2

...vertiser

...TONIC RIVER VALLEY

WEATHER FORECAST —
Today. Mostly sunny, high 71.
Tomorrow. Showers possible, 68.
A RETURN TO FAIR WEATHER

...MBER 18, 1926

PRICE FIVE CENT...

...Y

...btedly
...d and
...eloped
...n over
...north
...n the
...States
...n this
...chief
...oints
...f the
...m. It
...noted
...The
...n the
...River
...gion,

...that
...sity
...eral
...rty-
...the
...hat
...day
...rd,
...ure
...the
...The
...ne,
...rn
...es.
...he
...pi
...s.
...gs
...ht
...y
...d

VESSEL TORCHED IN INNSMOUTH HARBOR

On the morning of September 17, the Miskatonic County Fire Department responded to the report of a fire in the town of Innsmouth. Upon arrival on the scene, fire department officials found a derelict ship burning in the harbor. The nearest US Coast Guard station in Newburyport was contacted by telephone, but the commander of the station stated that no vessels could be deployed due to breaking wave conditions across the mouth of the Merrimac River. Several local fishermen were approached by the fire department, but declined to assist. When asked why, fire department officials were told that the fire had been set intentionally by the owners of the derelict vessel, and they would not interfere with their wishes to destroy their own property.

With no other property, vessels, or persons at risk from the fire, fire department officials decided to observe only. The blaze persisted for several hours, burning the derelict vessel to the waterline, at which point the fire was extinguished by seawater flooding the wreck. No one was injured, but the question remained of why the vessel was intentionally set ablaze. This reporter asked Fire Chief William Doughtery if any reason was given for the setting of the blaze. The following was his answer.

"At first we suspected the arson was a[n] attempt to collect insurance money, which is, of course, a crime, but a member of the Marsh family, the owners of the derelict vessel, the "Greta Mae," a former fishing trawler converted into a minelayer during the Great War, told us a convincing and worrisome tale. It seems that the vessel was uninsured, abandoned by its owners after it was unintentionally grounded shortly after the war during the worldwide effort to clear the seas of military munitions, and claimed as salvage by the Marsh family. The vessel had six defused sea mines aboard when she was grounded, and the munitions were never taken off. The Marsh family spokesman said that early yesterday morning thieves broke into the ship and were trying to steal one of the diffused mines, though for what purpose he couldn't say. He did say that several members of the Marsh family tried to intervene. The thieves fled, and when pursued, shot at and damaged the Marsh's boat. They didn't file a police report, so there's no way to corroborate their account. They said they burned the vessel to ensure that none of the munitions got into the wrong hands. No charges will be filed."

CONTINUED ON PAGE 2

Cleanup after Nor'Easter Continues

Many Miskatonic Valley homes and businesses continued the laborious process of cleaning up...

...when heavy rains and wind slammed the coast. Governor Alvan T. F...

GE 2

TORC

The burning hulk of the "Greta Mae" as witnessed throughout the day of September 17. Sadly, the nearby rainstorms never ventured close enough to extinguish the flames.

A worrisome tale indeed, and one that leaves this reporter wondering who might want to steal a military mine capable of sinking a ship, and why they might want one. Crime in our country is running rampant, with bootleggers, mobsters, and thugs terrorizing common citizens and flouting the law at every turn. This reporter dares not to speculate what might have happened if the Marsh family hadn't intervened, at the risk of their own lives and expense of their own property?

The people of Innsmouth are private folk, quiet and unassuming, wary of strangers, but with a deep sense of community and family. Perhaps we could all take a lesson from these fine citizens, watch out for our neighbors, speak up when something amiss is seen, and report any unfamiliar persons or suspicious activity. The police can't be everywhere at once, after all, and even Hoover's G-men can't catch all the gangsters and goons who mean to sell their poison and corrupt our children.

This reporter finds it comforting to know there are people in the world like the Marshes, who will stand up and do the right thing when the lawless threaten our lives and livelihoods.

LOCAL BEACHCOMBER FINDS "SEA MONSTER"

While beachcombing on Salisbury Beach after the recent nor'easter, a local fisherman, Warren Barton, discovered some grisly and rather disturbing remains washed up on the shore. What Mr. Barton initially thought to be the carcass of a seal, turned out to be something else entirely, but exactly what, we may never know.

Scant details were available, but Mr. Barton insisted that the remains were "nothing I ever seen before, and nothing I ever want to see again," and sported at least one human hand. The Newburyport Police, and Dr. Wallberg, the local medical examiner, were summoned to the scene, and this is where the story becomes somewhat obscured.

The police declined to make a formal statement for our paper, but one officer who was called to the scene, whose name we have withheld at his request, did tell us that the remains seemed to have been badly damaged. "Something had a bite of it, that's sure enough, and there wasn't much left. No head, one arm. The hand I saw sure enough looked human to me, but the rest... Dr. Wallberg's got a tough job, he does, trying to figure out who that was."

We were told that the remains were taken for examination, but were not allowed to see them for ourselves or take any photographs. Dr. Wallberg did, however, give us an interview, and, after conducting his examination, gave us this statement:

"The remains are in an advanced state of decomposition, which makes them difficult to Identify. Despite Mr. Barton's uneducated opinion, they are not some kind of sea monster, but the remains of a man and a large fish, both of which were consumed and partially digested by another larger predator, perhaps a shark or whale. The human remains were separated from those of the fish to the best of my ability, and will receive proper burial. The identity of the deceased will never be known. It's possible that a small fishing vessel was lost at sea in the recent storm, or the man fell overboard and drowned or came to perish some other way. He could even have fallen into the river far upstream, to be swept out to sea on the falling tide. There were significant signs of trauma, including broken bones and severe lacerations. The other remains were incinerated."

The US Coast Guard commandant informed our paper that no vessels were reported lost at sea during the days of the storm, and no mariners were reported lost at sea from any merchant ships or fishing craft. One of our sources, however, tracked down Mr. Barton and got a wholly different account of what he found on that beach.

"I been fishing these waters, man and boy, for fifty years, and I never seen anything like what I found on that beach. I combed that beach during the War, and I helped put dozens of men to rest who were lost at sea and washed up there, some half chewed up by sharks and what not. This wasn't a man. Men don't have webbing between their fingers like a frog, and scales instead of skin, nor claws like a cat. No, this weren't no man, and it weren't no part of a man. I know what I saw."

The Newburyportnews' source did mention that Mr. Barton appeared to have been drinking when he gave this account, and perhaps his memory was addled by spirits. The newspaper

Salisbury Beach, after the mysterious remains were removed by local authorities. This reporter also noted a terrible stench that remained long after the bodies were gone.

will not venture an opinion as to what, exactly, Mr. Barton found on Salisbury Beach, but we find the professional opinion of a physician more credible than that of an inebriated fisherman.

The remains of the poor lost soul, whoever he was, were buried in the Newburyport Cemetery in a grave marked only with a plain stone engraved with the date and the single word, "Unknown," which is, perhaps, the most accurate epitaph one could assign.